THE OLD POET'S TALE

BOOKS BY CARL RAKOSI

Two Poems (Modern Editions Press: New York, [1933])

Selected Poems (New Directions: Norfolk, Connecticut, [1941])

Amulet (New Directions: New York, 1967)

Ere-Voice (New Directions: New York, 1971)

Ex Cranium, Night (Black Sparrow Press: Los Angeles, 1975)

My Experiences in Parnassus (Black Sparrow Press: Los Angeles, 1977)

Droles de Journal (Toothpaste Press: West Branch, Iowa, 1981)

History (Oasis Books: London, 1981)

Spiritus, I (Pig Press: Durham, England, 1983)

The Collected Prose of Carl Rakosi
(National Poetry Foundation: Orono, Maine, 1983)

The Collected Poems of Carl Rakosi
(National Poetry Foundation: Orono, Maine, 1986)

The Beasts (Margery Cantor & Friends: Oakland, California, 1994 [1995])

Poems 1923-1941 (Sun & Moon Press: Los Angeles, 1995)

The Earth Suite (etruscan books: Buckfastleigh, Devonshire, 1997)

CARL RAKOSI

THE OLD POET'S TALE

etruscan books

1999

First published by etruscan books

The Old Poet's Tale copyright © Callman Rawley, 1999
This edition world copyright © etruscan books, 1999

COPYRIGHT

etruscan books
24a Fore Street
Buckfastleigh
South Devonshire TQ11 0AA

ISBN 1 901538 14 1
ISBN 1 901538 21 4 (cased)
Printed in an edition of 700 copies (paper) and 100 (cased); the first 26 copies lettered
A – Z by Carl Rakosi with additional holograph material.

etruscan books is a member of the Association of Little Presses.
Its books are distributed by S.P.D., 1341 7th Street, Berkeley CA, 94710 USA and available from
Collected Works, 1st Floor, Flinders Way Arcade, 238 Flinders Lane, Melbourne 3000, Australia and
Peter Riley (Books), 27 Sturton Street, Cambridge CB1 2QG, UK

etruscan books are edited by Nicholas Johnson.
Set by R.W Palmer at Tuff Talk Press, Bath.
Printed at Short Run Press, Exeter.

CONTENTS

In the Constellation

The Old Poet's Tale

Meditations

Satyricon

Drôles de Journal (1924 –

Poet's Corner

For Andrew Crozier

IN THE CONSTELLATION

SONG

Let the morning pursue me
with the wind that senses her body.
Let the clouds carry my message.
Then might she yield.

Lying in the constellation of The Bear,
have pity, gazelle, on him who must fly
to the stars to reach you.

After Jehudah Halevi

EVERYMAN

copulate
          < copulare:
to join,
          to couple.
Says nothing
          of lust,
the iron master,
          sweaty,
breathless,
          fierce.

THE HUSBAND

There were many things
to watch:
        her teeth
her heart
        her weight
her nipples
        the albumen
in her water,
        finally
her shoes
        no longer fit.

So took her hand:
"Your looks
are not gone.

Take it easy.
You'll know
when your time comes
and will not have a Mongolian
idiot in the taxi.

We'll make it
even if I have to tie
the cord myself."

THE ARRIVAL

*"Thou art the rudeliest welcome
to this world that ever was."*
Pericles

I felt the foetus
stir a foot
below my wife's breast

and woke the neighbours
with my shouting.

O first born, listen!
I am your provider.

Let us get
to know each other!

LEAH

Belial my oaf warned me
she would not be
                        suitable for a poem...
bedded and tongued
                        together too long.

She does not belong
                        to my ulcerous
subliminal.
                  She is natural.
She runs off
                  like rain water.
I could not put her
                        under the hard master
of an image
                  for my own need.

So since poetry
                        is more abstract,
more for its registrar,
                              give me her smile
and let us hug
                        and romp
in the plain life

or I am lost!

THE MÉNAGE

Up stand
   six
yellow
   jonquils
in a
  glass/
the stems
   dark green,
paling
   as they descend
into the water/
     seen through
a thicket
   of baby's breath, "a tall herb
bearing numerous small,
       fragrant white flowers."
I have seen
   snow-drops larger.
I bent my face down.
     To my delight
they were convoluted
    like a rose.
They had no smell,
    their white
the grain of Biblical dust,
     which like the orchid itself
is as common as hayseed.
     Their stems were thin and woody
but as tightly compacted
    as a tree trunk,
greenish rubbings showing in spots
      through the brown;

wiry, forked twigs so close,
                       they made an impassable bush
which from a distance
              looked like mist.

I could barely escape
                  from that wood of particulars...
the jonquils whose air within
                     was irradiated topaz,
silent as in an ear,
              the stems leaning lightly
against the glass,
              trisecting its inner circle
in the water,
            crossed like reverent hands
(ah, the imagination!
                Benedicite.
Enter monks.
          Oops, sorry!
Trespassing
         on Japanese space.
Exit monks
         and all their lore
from grace).

I was moved by all this
              and murmured
to my eyes, "Oh, Master!"
                and became engrossed again
in that wood of particulars
                until I found myself
out of character, singing
    "Tell me why you've settled here."

"Because my element is near."
and reflecting,
                    "The eye of man cares. Yes!"

But a familiar voice
                    broke into the wood,
a shade of mockery in it,
                    and in her smile
a fore-knowledge
                    of something playful,
something forbidden,
                    something make-believe
something saucy,
                    something delicious
about to pull me
                    off guard:
"Do you want to be my Cupid-o?"

In fairness to her
                    it must be said
that her freckles
                    are always friendly
and that the anticipation
                    of a prank
makes them radiate
                    across her face
the way dandelions
                    sprout in a field
after a summer shower.

"What makes you so fresh,
                    my Wife of Bath?
What makes you so silly,
                    o bright hen?"

"That's for you to find out,
                         old shoe, old shoe.
That's for you to find out
                     if you can."

"Oh yeah!"
               (a mock chase and capture).
"Commit her
               into jonquil's custody.
She'll see a phallus
               in the pistil.
Let her work it off there."

But I was now myself
               under this stringent force
which ended,
               as real pastorals in time must,
in bed, with the great
               eye of man, rolling.

THE FATHER

I find among my notes
a crayon drawing
of a prancing pony
with pink and blue legs

and an upright endpiece
looking more like a black
bush than a tail.

The eyes are bull's eyes,
fierce white in a black ring.

There is no mistaking
two rudimentary horns,
pink also, protruding
from the forehead.

This is mitigated
by an assortment of red
and pink cookie-shapes
spangled over the pony's coat
and by a green box saddled to his middle
with a pink ribbon

on which you had printed
when you were four years old
HAPPY BIRTHDAY

forgetting that on the other side
you had scribbled
MOMMY IS A DOPE!

Which reminds me of the pact
you tried to make
after announcing you were
sipping sopping soaking wet:

"When I do something bad
I'll tell you how to punish me."

No dice.

Animal charm?
               You bet.
Viz., "Here, little egg,
I want to eat you!"

But I'll never understand
what made you say,
"I'm tired of being four,
I want to be five."

Where to, Mistress Quickly?

QUESTIONS FOR JENNIFER EBIN, MY EIGHTEEN-MONTH OLD GRANDDAUGHTER

Whose face is so fair
that her eyes look blue
though they are brown

and bubbles fresh
and sits in me
like a nut in a shell?

Who knows, are we a galaxy
or a familial cell?

In what Sumerian babble,
wrapped for the night in a dark crib,
does she re-enact the hilarious encounter
with her body in the warm bath
and dada the dog
and bapa the grandpa
and her first complete sentence:
"Bye bye bubble down drain?"

Who is the inane reader
holding up one finger,
asking, "How much is one finger?"

Who bleeds for time
yet runs with her
into a bubble
and finds it interesting?

He who is without onus probandi,
a grandfather
(grandmothers will have to write
their own riddles).

MORALITY PLAY,
EARLY

From observing
          mother
and herself
          while talking
she discovered
          she could talk
to herself
          and concluded
there were two
          of her,
the one
     to help the other.
The voice
     must come
with its own
          stage then,
but the characters,
          she knew,
were up to her.

At two
     she tried out
her first
     person.
The voice
     said,
"I am not bad."

THE ELDER SISTER

When she was four
a sister cooed
and took her mother.

What is mine?
was then her question.
End of innocence.

She knew now
she was envious
and overbearing.

God, how she wept
and hated then,
yet looked at me

as if to ask,
"Why are you
sad?

Come into my room.
I'll hide my pain
and we'll play."

EVENING WITH MY GRANDDAUGHTERS

o for a world with a string and a kitten
and Tipsy who loves us so much
                                    he pees
and you and I.

TO MY GRANDDAUGHTERS' HOUSE

There is a hegemony
                    of mother
where the cucumber is real
but between my house
                    and yours
null turns into Titania
and a star
            is not literal.

SERVICES

There was a man in the land of Ur.

Who's that at my coattails?
A pale cocksman.

Hush!
The rabbi walks in thought
                              as in an ordained measure
to the Ark
              and slowly opens its great doors.
The congregation rises
                        and faces the six torahs
and the covenant
                    and all beyond.
The Ark glows.
              Hear, O Israel!

The rabbi stands before the light
inside, alone, and prays.
It is a modest prayer
for the responsibilities of his office.
The congregation is silent.

I too pray:
Let Leah my wife be recompensed for her sweet smile
and our many years of companionship
and not stick me when she cuts my hair.
And let her stay at my side at large gatherings.
And let my son George and his wife Leanna
and my daughter Barbara be close,

and let their children, Jennifer, Julie, Joanna and Miriam
be my sheep
        and I their old shepherd.
Let them remain as they are.

And let not my white hair frighten me.

The tiger leaps,
the baboon cries,
Pity, pity.
The rabbi prays.

There was a man in the land of Ur.

I, son of Leopold and Flora,
also pray:
I pray for meaning.
I pray for the physical,
for my soul needs no suppliant.
I pray for man.

And may a special providence look out
for those who feel deeply.

THE GLASS OF MADEIRA

Madeira,
>   you have put me
into a null state.
>   Now I know
what the Eskimo meant
>   when he said
"The weather is our master."

I know, you want me
>   in a kind of interval,
or heavy water.
>   Another glass
and I'll be your placebo.

Well, I feel no pain.
>   I'll rest awhile
in this ancient limbic system.
If I sit here long enough,
>   I may figure out
the gravitational pull
>   of words:
viz., "The sea is old
>   but the earth is older."

The vine from which you came
>   was brought from Cyprus
by the Portuguese
>   to the island of Madeira
where the green canary abounds
and sixhundredninetyfive species of beetles.
The coast is rocky
>   and the sea unquiet,
hence there are few algae.
The rock is basalt
>   of volcanic origin,

dark and hard.
There are few meadows and pastures.
The cattle feed on the mountains,
and on the lower slopes
                              are a few towns.

This is said
                    to reassure
men of facts
                    dragging an ass.

Good Madeira,
                    let me lie in your glass
in the mellow quality
                              of latency.
Do not unlock us.
                    The cubic light
of a small planet
                    left its source
at the time of Prospero,
                              iron-red,
and entered here.

                    What time is this?
The axis of the earth inclines,
                              the fish swims to the hook,
the old man plants
                    a plum tree for his granddaughter.

Profound Madeira,
                    let me get some of this pressure
off my bladder.
                    I'm stoned.
I don't know my backbone
                              from a tuning fork.
Don't anybody
                    bump my arm
or try to stop me.

Undefinably deep and strange
                    is this lighted enclave,
this underwater amber,
like the words of a philosopher
                    with a taste for style:

"There is a mustard seed
                    in the shape of the earth.
But it doesn't matter."

In this condition
                    it is easy to be deceived.
The last words
                    of Beethoven on his death bed,
after four operations,
                    "Too late! Too late!"
also looked profound
                    until the reference was traced
to a shipment of his favorite Rhine wine.

Verily, I slobber over.
It wouldn't surprise me
                    if four mink
dashed across this scene,
                    pulling an orange crate.
I wouldn't bat an eye.

What's the matter?
Don't we peasants
                    deserve to be entertained?

I'm not going to budge
                    from this love seat
until Leah calls.

LYING IN BED ON A SUMMER MORNING

How pleasant are the green
and brown tiles
of my neighbour's roof.
The branches of his elm tree
stretch across
and make a delightful
composition,
                        the angle
of the roof
                        the exact plane
which the branch needs
to be interesting.
Le mot juste? la branche juste!

And you, my dark spruce,
dominate the left side
of this composition.
You are clannish but authentic
and stand, uncompromising,
for the family of trees.

And all at once the early birds
all break out chirping
as when the bidding opens
on the stock exchange.
                        Then one,
the long sweet warble
of a finch.
                        Oh stay!
And then a chant from down the street,
two boys triumphant,
very small in thick glasses:
"We got a bird nest! We got a bird nest!"

A contrary air.
                    It is gone.
And the blue sky,
                    clear as in Genesis,
holds.

What is there between us?
an abstract air...
a state sans question
                    or inquietude...
something light
                    as a country air
yet serious as gold
or man sui generis.

GINGER

Am I the only one
                watching
my neighbour's
                frolicksome goat,
Ginger,
        tied to a pecan tree?
All morning
            it has been examining
an empty bushel basket
                    and has lifted
one leg delicately
                like a circus horse
as if to roll it,
            but whether to do that
or to butt it
            with its small horns,
that is the question.
                    Not of great moment,
no signing of the Charter,
                    but like air music,
quickest of the elements.
                    Towards which I leaped!

In form
        its own grace,
appearing,
            as it passed
in retrospect, classical.

The real goat stayed,
                    imperturbable,
the body solid
            as a four-square loom

and delivered me
                    from abstraction.
His coloring,
                    greyish-soft shades,
their dark and light
                    passing into each other
as in an antique rubbing.

I now found myself
                    sitting so near,
my shade,
                    as in the Inferno,
sensed his,
                    but he gave no sign
of my presence,
                    even when I stroked him
and my heart leaped
                    at the gentle fleece,
too fine for a hard life.
He continued nibbling
                    on a dry bush.

I would not have believed
                    unconcern
could bolster the man in me
                    and be so enduring.
Sic transit, not caring
                    whether it is recognized,
the Divine
                    (from another age).

He was poking
                    into the underbush now
and reached across my head
                    for the small spiny twigs.

At that the phase
                 changed
and a sensuous trembling
                              hung in the air,
as when a bee is about
                     to descend
on blossoming clover,
                    and I
felt myself being pulled
                     as by a line
from the invisible
                  other side
to enter goathood,
                   deeper than sight.

LITTLE GIRLS ON THE PHONE

"Will you talk
        to Amy,
grandpa?"

Low whisperings.
        Suddenly the voices turn harsh,
drill sergeants arguing,
          criss-crossing, peremptory orders
under a hush.
        Amy refuses!

Lucky for me, hickory nut.
          Last time
you sprang at me
        with a laugh,
chanting:
        "Happy birthday to you.
        You live in a zoo.
        You look like a monkey
        and you act like one too."

Why should I remember this now
          with such tenderness?

Good bye, chipmunk.
Stay in your capital.

TO A COLLIE PUP

Nobody had to show you
where the sun is
or that my back
could serve the same purpose
as a tree.

Why, you are hardly old enough
to know the difference
between your tail and a shadow,
yet the warm radiator
and your bowl of water
are already old friends.

The way you look up at me
with a saint in each eye
one would never suspect
that you chase birds
and chickens and steal stale bread
from the neighbour's trashcan.

Lay off, you beggar,
I just fed you
and took you walking.

Go spring
into the autumn leaves.
Nuzzle and roll
as if there were nothing
in the whole wide world
but fun.

How is it
that you play
with my shoelace
and understand so well
how to love me?

For this you shall have
the key to my bedroom
and the degree
of master of arts.

IN A WARM BATH

Buddha is not more strange
                        and impersonal
than you, o belly
                    waiting for the doctor's probe,
or you, phallus
                    wrinkled as an old crocodile
in a salt marsh.
                                Horn of schlemiel!
Uxorious! Imperative! Boaster! Father!
Outside the order of imagination
                    and the public interest.

Father! In what way father? Too old.
                    Can't tell him though.
Nor he me. Too much pain in the eyes.
His black obsidian gaze is closed to me
(may be just light refracted).
                                        Why closed?

He can be fond and amiable.
Dangerous to press for more.

Engage in argument. God help me!
Like an owl zeroing in on a mouse
aware too late of its exposure
he breaks from ambush with transfixing logic.

Yet he is sympathetic.
The clarity I taught him
he has turned against me
and I am satisfied.

I say a man has integrity.
For this he cares. And I.
Looks at me long and deep,
a straight beam unavoidable.
And I to him.
I was made father for this.

Eyes clasped,
            down we go into a mine
without a guide or map,
and damn the pinched face
            of the Puritan
who holds us back.

Be careful though in table talk,
hold in the thought, "When I am gone..."
though all I mean is fact, faceless.
Can't bear to see him laid low.
Careful not to give him pain,
I swear it as a father,
until the time when he and I
must put the figurative
            prayer shawl
on together and join Abraham.

Inventor of the wheel,
            save us from cancer.

Bless this water.
            I must bathe more often.

THE CODE

I had to pull the little maple tree
close to the house.
                    It had leaves already
and I saw a doe standing
                    in its romaunt
munching peacefully
                    while the wolf stalked.
Such is my confusion.

When I broke it,
only the moloch *unthink*
                    groaned.

The seed knew
            before Sinai
it would be a root
            but not the nature
of man.

It was coded
            to become a shade tree
sized for the Colossus
                    Rameses the Second
and entered the earth
                    zigzagging
after the radish and the worm.
Its necessity would have cracked my cement
and pierced a water main.
Yet it was coded
            in the presence of the sun
to turn our breath and water
                    into deer food

and connect us to our nature
and give us peace from pursuance.

In our deadly assignation
I was coded to be contemplative
with a twig:
                "out of the ground
only an hour,
                    yet so downcast.
Poor Yorick!"

In the root I saw a miniature
                    crab-apple tree
twisting into Dada.
                    Insane ending.

Must all lead back to the thinker?
                            Is there no
germination in a cube
                    or sprouting in a sphere?

THE NIGHT BUS

Great wheels.
                    Better step back.
Like standing next to a pyramid.

Scale.
                Not much used
yet mighty.
                "On the scale of my life,"
a thought,
            as if I had heard
a voice.
                Instantly
the elements slip into place:
my house, the rocks, the ocean.
Is this their night orbit?
This is not where they were.

Country road
                under the headlights
speeding, beautiful,
glances off my cheek,
an abstract flow.

Burrr. The tires
as from a Scot glottis.
Gurgling then
                but soft and long,
unrolling,
            rubber slapping softly
against the cement,
the driver's foot asleep.

Dark bus body.
>   Night, the *ursprache*.
Gold out of quiet
>   light around him.
No, it is more delicate,
more like an emanation
>   a man
alone
>   longing.
Of my eyes
>   yet outside,
a cousin to the strange,
the lovely Elizabethan line,
"We have the receipt of fern-seed,
we walk invisible."

But voices interevene:
"I get antsy. I have to stretch my legs,
get out into a trout stream."

Deeply comforting, the ordinary,
but I contract into a cricket's pulse
and have to travel through my medium
on a higher frequency.

Night.
>   Where am I?
In a dense Bartokian wood
sans entropy,
tactile with frogs,
conceivably a negative of space,
yet starts felicity.
Here am I absolutely tuned.
Call Titania to my side
for Leah cannot follow me here.

Here sometimes there is no way in
except by some other poet's bungling.
Then I cry out,
      "Not that way, this way!"
and I find myself in the wood again
and all is well.

Then an old voice
      as from a balcony,
a lady,
   sweet:
"Mother always impressed on us
that never was a long time,"
referring to her own rebelliousness,
and she ought at least to try.

The way of the world:
the old are wise,
the young think they know.
This is her magic wood,
I must not mock it.

Then another:
"I gotta go back
and look under a leaf
like when I was a kid to see
if I'm really a sensitive loner
or just an image."

Intellectual. Laughs.
I refuse to look pleased
or contend with his intellect.
All I want is to reach out
and touch his hand.

48

Who is that staring at me?
Cold eye of a pragmatist,

                      my ancient enemy.

Well, if a dog in time
can look like its master,
why not the eyes of a pragmatist,
from always fixing on a practical object,
come to look that hard?

But lutes hang in the air

                      unplayed.
The poet plots an axis

                  in space
and Leah becomes my polestar.

A TABLET AGAINST AGING

You are as fixed in me,

                o loyal wife,

as the bright

           point of Canopus

to the helmsman.

YOU

in whom distrust lies
    like a gallstone
and desire grows up aching,
    a sharp tooth,
there are times your courage
    rises over all
and knows no high airs
    or aloofness.

Then I plant myself near you
and swear I shall never leave.

YOUNG COUPLES STROLLING BY

When we get a good day here
                              the bee is at meridian
and little girls in worn-out slippers
charm the adversary
                    in the stranger's eye.

Incognito then enters
                      the coupling influence of the sun
licking an ice cream cone
and Swedes become Italians
                          and Italians become lizards
and Diogenes goes sailing.

YOUNG GIRL

on her way to the beach,
walking daintily in bare feet
to avoid the stones.

Titania's gauze
forms a cute skirt
              so short
it takes the breath away
and opens in front
to admit man
to her shapely legs
                walking brightly
in inexorable scissor movement
through his child taboos.

At thirteen she
already swings her hips
ostensibly to keep her balance
and re-enacts the secret
of man's bed.
She smiles and shoots
implacable seduction
straight into the eyes.

A nimbus envelops her girdle.

O stay!

Disclose your meaning.

"I like the way you look at me,
the lubricities of your mind."

Hold it, grandpa.
From where I stood, it sounded more like
"How delightful
that you noticed my new swimming suit!
It makes me feel like a woman."

Touché!

But was it so far out to imagine
that in the safety of that dark,
rather old-fashioned, sensitive
homuncio look in the poet's eyes,
having only a moment,
she let the panther out
of her pubic lair
to show that she was nubile
and became ionized herself?

It was a great day
for Patrick Henry
                    Junior High.

Such bitter-sweet discombobulations
in a moment turn men into Pierrots.

SIXTEEN, A TRANCE-LIKE POLARITY

full voluptuous lips,
                    the other pole
a far-away look,
                    the eyes pure hazel.
Voluptas
            in the inner city,
the eyes
            forbidden to show it.
They had fled
                    to the north
to remain chaste
                    and cool
and to escape
                    public disaster,
for there had been
                    an uprising
(but of that
            no glimpse)
and she had been
                    surprised and taken,
inaccessible loveliness
                    and all,
transient,
            unbearably moving.

Two years later
                    the eyes were clear
and confident
                    and held me firmly,
the teeth larger,
                    the face strong.
A peasant had moved in.

TIME TO KILL

a man and his dog

what fun
chasing twigs
into the water!

young girls bicycle by
in pairs and plaid shorts

a wind so soft
one's whole
back tingles
with cilia

a gentle lake

the sun boils
at the center,
radiates the zone
for man
            and lays
a healing pad
across his nape

an airplane small and flat
as a paper model
roars behind
the Virgilian scene

an old man tips
his straw hat
down to shade
                    his eyes,
pulls up his fishline
and moves on
to a new spot

the poor small
wood louse
crawls along
the bark ridge
for his life

SHORE LINE

We speak of *mankind*.
Why not *wavekind*?

Barrel-chested military water
rushes in a mass
to break the shore earth
into *stonekind*.

Pphlooph pphlooph
                    the waves grope
indistinctly for the shore.

As delicate
            as a butterfly
along a cheek
                a boat with white
and orange sail appears.
A small boy in a life-belt
sits in front and looks ahead
with all his might.
                    His father steers,
attached like a shaft
to his son's safety
and the sail's management.

A sunfish thrown back by a fisherman
lies drowned and pitching.
The eyes are white in death.

This is the raw data.
A mystery translates it
into feeling and perception;
then imagination;

finally the hard
inevitable quartz
figure of will
      and language.

Thus a squirrel tail flying
from a handlebar
unmistakably establishes
its passing rider
as a male unbowed
      in a chipper plume.

JIG, YOU WINE BUMS

bite the hard cool
　　　　　　apple of the air!

The season of muscatel has come
when the squirrel   runs
up the tree fornicating
and the deer bolts

and man reaches
for his calking gun
and paint brush

and the middle aged hiker
throws his shoulders back.
Look at him go!

This is lavender and rose
time in drawers

when the sun is cooler but more blinding
and the maple leaves distill its light
into a cheerful red liqueur.

Now, wine bums,
the winter is long.
Elixir falls from the air
and even the misanthrope
　　　　　　　　　　's eye twinkles
in the commonplace.

NASTURTIUM

a flower of a name!
An exquisite self

rooted in the God
in the earth

like man. My eyes
are in an aria.

Oh for a metaphor
from the brain of Sappho!

IN THE FALL

When the apple is on the tree
and the moth's work is done

and tots with runny noses
dawdle on their way to school

and the goose is in
his fall plumage

and the duck hunter
waits in the early morning,
shivering in his dark boat

and the smell of burning
leaves is in the air

and the summer screens
have been taken down

and the father is teaching his
young son how to catch a ball

and couples rush to
restaurants and plays

before winter drives the pheasant
and the pensioner south,

this is when bats fly
and so do I.

SPRING FANTASY

There goes Basho,
balls and all,
into the pond again.

Splashes, *Plophh!*
like an old frog.

Must be Spring,
and I'm in a small
mode of music

through a phonograph
cartridge.

Solid briar root,
varnish,
beetle's chitin

enter soundlessly
as a mystique
into Orfeo's

perfect system,
passing on a stylus
from the earth

into art.

IN THE WOODS

At night the little stream
under the old footbridge
gurgles and tremoloes over the pebbles.
Then a murmuring,
                            then silence.

Aeons pass

                    Nothing moves!

The silence of the dark!

Suddenly a small splash.
                            A fish?

A loner in the stillness.

Then again leaves swish
in the light wind
and the rivulet flows
downstream, sucking and gurgling,
and bats swarm from the dark
into all directions.

The woods are having their night,
and I heard a voice :
My Name Is Master Of Reality.
I Have An Assignation With Thy Nature.

WHAT'S IN A NAME?

Here's *Dogwood.*

The constable?

No! *Cornus Florida,*
a tree whose red berries
feed *Turdus Orpheus,*
the finest warbler in the woods.

And what's *Sneezeweed?*
            Ragwood?
            Burdock?

The Merry Wives of Windsor?

ELIZABETHAN PSALM

Farnaby's at his lute again.

Exultate Deo!

"IN THY SLEEP/
LITTLE SORROWS SIT AND WEEP"

In the night
a little crow
whose wing was broken
lay on the ground
and cried out.

Strigidae
the owl
protector of grain
heard
and glided
            soundless
nearby to a low branch.

Straight ahead he looked
like a man
            engraved
as on an
            ancient
measuring cup
or seated at
            the knee
of Michelangelo's *Night*
waiting
            motionless
erect.

Not two weeks old
the crow slept.

An hour passed.
A feather stirred.

Instantly the great
head swivelled
and the bird of prey
                    leaped
spearing
and carried off the body
to a distant tree stump.

Again he waited
                    listening.
The implacable beak
then grasped it
by the head
and gulped it down.
Three times
he swallowed,
spitting out
the crow bones,
fur and feathers.

Then the great bird
silent
on Egyptian tombs
blinked
preened
and hooted.

68

POEM

The ants came
to investigate
the dead
bull snake,
nibbled
at the viscera
and hurried off
with full mouths
waving wild
antennae.

Moths alighted,
beetles swarmed,
flies buzzed
in the stomach.

Three crows
tugged and tore
and flew off
to their oak tree
with the skin.

In every house
men, women and children
were chewing beef.

Who was it said,
"The wonder of the world
is its comprehensibility"?

THE OLD POET'S TALE

PRELUDE

At Stagira lies Saint Belle
and there lies also the body of Aristotle.
And you shall understand
that her bones are anointed
with the gum of plum trees
and that all men are used
to attend her grave on Lent.

And men say that in her youth
she was led into a garden of Caiaphas
and there she was crowned
with the sweet thorn called barbariens.

But now this is no more
but a tablet seven cubits long
above her head
on which the title is written
in Hebrew, Greek and Latin
and the date
when it was laid in the earth.

And the body of Aristotle
stinks too in a casket
at Stagira but the eyes
are in Paris in the king's chapel.
Yet the emperor of Almayne
claims he has them,
and I have often seen them,
but they are greater
than those in Paris.

CHRONICLE

At first the hair
grew thicker on his chest
and stomach,

then gray appeared
along the right side

and one day
in the mirror
he saw a gray bush
in his nostrils

and took his teeth out
from the water glass
and cut himself
a little sausage.

As a boy
he had been in a hurry
to get older.

PROBLEMS OF THE AGED

"You look remarkably young."

I? The old mandrake root?

"The white hair
                    has not reached your genitals yet!"

"What do you do all day?"

I plant radishes, you damn fool!

And hang around doctors' offices,
                                    medical hands on me,
waiting for the report.

And crack jokes:
                "I don't deserve this.
I've been faithful to my wife!"

To whom can one turn?

"She was a great beauty in her youth
and came from a distinguished family."

What is the earthly point of that?

The unrelenting eyes spoke:
"You knew you were going to be old.
Why didn't you prepare for it?"

Well, I have had kindnesses.

                        But the inexorable!

That's only good

               for making eyes compassionate.

So there's a scale

               to the rest of me.

Who is there

               to carry that burden?

And a dew drop

               to collect my affinity

for earth.

Merde!

THE HISTORY OF MAN

That cry of agony
                    from a carious tooth,
the man from the age
                    of orogenies
has left his parameters here
and a memory
                    of his ordeal.

CONVERSATION IN A HOTEL ROOM

"When my time comes, I want to be out as usual on the playing field
with George and Homer, not in a hotel room
                              like the Chairman of the Conference.
I'd like it to be Sunday morning. The sun is shining.
On the ground beside me are my three favorite balls.
I pick one up and hold it for a moment
and look out over the bowling green
and as I get the bead and reach back to throw
I want to just buckle under, nice and easy, and stay down!"

This is a shepherd's song
a moment as authentic
as the State Flower of Iowa
when man with offices in eighteen cities but few words
reaches for the Old Crow
and discovers Tom Sawyer in The Financial World
(I had forgotten how much I miss Tom)
and I hear a shepherd singing:
How Endearing and Inscrutable is Man.

STREET TALK

How goes it,
old timer?

Like a cliché,
unobserved.

I've been rewritten
into modern language

and cooked
with the spices

of a personality
until hard-boiled

and I'm still me,
the same old shoe.

Like Satchel Paige,
I don't look back.

Something might be
gaining on me.

Note: Satchel Paige was a great African-American baseball
player, something of a legend in his time, and often quoted
for his pithy sayings.

THE SENIOR CITIZEN

The days are long.
The girl technicians chat
and laugh about their dates
as if there were no unknown
pensioner on the X-ray table.

The stud days are over.
In the morning you will see
                    only aged widows
at the cashier's window
                 patient pachidermal
waiting to pay an electric bill.

The money-making days are gone.
The day is long
            in the bird sanctuary
and the periodical room.

No more kidding around
               in the office.
It's *face the earth* now.

WALKERS PASSING EACH OTHER
IN THE PARK

Had I been eighty-five,
                    he would have stopped
to compare notes,
                    but what was there
to talk about
                    with a man only sixty-five?

OLD LOVERS

Bubeleh,
        if you will be
good-natured,
             I can be
wise.

THE DEAD FATHER

Let me be an old dog in a corner
or a pair of favorite slippers
                              by your bed
and hear again about your early life
and have you care for me forever.

DIARY

"Have you done
what I told you?"
asked my father
in a dream.

He had recommended
a methods book.

"No," I replied
in perfect French,
a language I can read
but not speak.

I was unusually composed
and in good spirits.

"Listen to the Hungarian!"
meaning me, he cried
to my mother, delighted,
then said it in French,
but it was unbelievably
heavy like interlocked
German gutturals
and took forever.

We all laughed.

Then the dream faded:
he was very old now
and spoke in a level tone
that was not his voice
but merely a semblance.

He was dead serious,
thinking about my welfare
and my needs.

Then a foreboding
like a shadow
crossed his mind,
that after he was gone,
I would remember that
he had really cared
and I would grieve.

He was sad.

I grieved and awoke then.

THE STREET

Like slag
        the face,
old,
one who knows he has been banished,
knows his place,
expects no sympathy or interest.

At seeing me
        the face
lit up at once
        and smiled,
expecting a smile:
           You're one of us!

AN AGELESS FACE

That gives the orbit.
The eyelids hang low
(low clearance),
dark and sad.
That's for utterance.

An undertaker left
his bags here.

All here.

HOW GOES IT WITH TIME?

The auditors have sent me notice.
There is not enough left in my account
to piss with

but what there is
will cure vanity
and end metastasis

and make a cabbage of me:
all my value will be under ground.

If I could look at it
I would not.

In short, it is all that matters.
The *ongenbite* of iron.
The rest can be learned.

THE OLD MAN'S HORNPIPE

This puppy jumping up
to reach the mouth
               of man

this running of little girls
                    like sandpipers
to get there before their thoughts do

this whippoorwill at the tail end of winter

ah, Atlantis!

THE OLD MAN DREW THE LINE

The old man
            drew the line
for his son,
            the executive:
"I don't want you spending money on me!
(not as long as there are fathers),"
the line ageless
                as the independence of time.
Musters tears
            and overflows
the inner ear,
                yet does not matter.
It can not cure frailty.

I seek him
            who will seek me out
and will believe
                what I do not believe
(that is my frailty).
                "Sit down here with us,"
he says,
            "You don't have to impress anyone.
Here is my hand.
                Your age is of no significance."
Ah!
    I move closer to his mouth
and look into his eyes.
                I do not avert mine,
there is no reason to,
                or retreat
into a kindly smile.

Ah, companero,
>
> you were born
on the wrong day
>
> when God was paradoxical.
You'll have to
>
> find yourself an old dog.

SHORT MEDITATION

Now that I am old,
must I give up
paradoxes and
crossed signals

and fish for poignancy
in a safe persona?

Is there no wisdom,
only common sense?

THE INCURABLE ILLNESS

I am ninety years old.
I don't think anymore.

                       It can't help me.

Who could look at me

                       lying here

and know what I was?

A woman sobbed in the passage.

AT THE OPEN CASKET

We had the same mother,
                    the same father,
walked the same streets.
                    Often we were waylaid
on our way to school
                    and would scrap side by side.
Our underclothes
                    with the fresh smell of soap
used to lie
          neatly folded
in the same drawer.

(Takes off his tie
                  and hands it to the undertaker)
"Put this on him.
          He was always neat."

In the end is the man
                    of flesh.
He leaped into the grave
                    for that principle.

His habits,
          too, were principles.
His voice as a man,
                  the warmth,
thick in phlegm
          far back of the palate.

The eyes
      looking inward

a light entering
                    like a pin head
as a comic memory
                        came into his mind.
His bearing, modest;
he was taken for ordinary.

How loveable he appears
                        from this distance!

In the end is the man
                of family.

I must look at him again.

The features are the same,
though less pinched, less nervous.
The color in his cheeks is fairly natural.
There's dignity the way he's stretched out.
Objective cancelled.
                        Out of work.
Lies as in a pause.
                        Very peaceful.
(I don't remember that!)

That's the undertaker's specialty.
The man's gone mad in physics,
                        I in metaphysics.

AT THE GRAVESIDE

Yes, I was old.
My colon had become as thin
                                as the middle finger.
The joints had swollen
                          into clenched fists.
I had stones
                the size of clinkers.
Leonardo dissected me
                      and was astonished
that they looked like iron.

There was a time
                      when I came to a place like this
and put on a special face too
                        and stood motionless,
thinking,
        "Only he can say,
'No more anxiety.
Never. Never. Never.'"

I had a way with words.

WHAT'S HIS OFFENSE?

He's young
and lies with women
                    in his imagination.
The apprehension of death
grips him by the neck.
He'll go as close to an old man
as to blubber
washed up on the beach.

What's his offense?

He will not look.
The face is too old.
He will not look.

THE OLD POET'S TALE

I   Character

I myself have never written
about the anguish
of death, for I write

only from experience
but now that I
have Alzheimer's Disease

the only serious subject
as in a mortuary
is mortality...........

and I weep!

There was no mystery
about my character
or working principles.

Already into the
disease, I said
to a young poet,

"Because you write
does not mean
a poetic impulse.

That remains
to be proved."

The curious
pertinacity
of character!

II   A Day in the Country

One by one
the young poets,
cautioned by my wife,

approached me
for a pleasant word,
then retreated,

I standing by myself,
my face clouded over,
and I replied politely.

How they bustled and
chatted, the wives
setting the tables

laying out the cheeses
for a picnic
the men in a huddle

by themselves
drinking beer,
good Joe's.

How so light-hearted
as if carrying
a high note inside?

Care-free too?
Must be the outdoors
and the idea

of a picnic.
A case of summer
ungluing poets.

Bless the everyday.
"This is the weather
the cuckoo likes

and so do I."
And Bruegel:
come out, peasants,

pick your beau
swing your partners
and doe-si-doe

never mind that
I'm tied to a post
like a dog waiting

for his mistress
to reappear
with the mustard

while the fiddles
tear up the air,
damn the Alzheimer,

hold on, Flo,
whirl to the right
and let 'er go.

III   The Destination

In the biblical vapors
light appeared
and it was morning

and the time had come
to take me to
The Home For The Aged.

I had never seen
my poor wife so downcast
and quiet, her eyes

set where I was not,
her jaws clenched,
unnatural the whole house.

Thus we set out,
she driving,
I strapped in.

On the way
a familiar figure
joined us,

greeting me
as if I were
an old acquaintance.

I knew the face,
the eyes in particular,
unaccountably attendant,

(from somewhere)
but not the name
nor why he was there.

I'll call him
Shade, trustworthy
Shade, my *he*.

As I approached
his identity, however,
I lost my way

while they chatted
about nothing
out of the ordinary

as if to show
they were ingenuous,
not to worry, etc.,

but I had no stomach
for such words
and it was lost on me.

We were both aware now
of each other
without looking

when in that frame
I heard THE SCREAM
by Edvard Munch

but could not tell
from whose mouth
it was vomiting,

we were so close.

The next thing I knew
the talking had stopped.
We had reached

our destination,
The Home For The Aged
and a dead silence.

Reluctantly my poor wife
and the reliable Shade
carried my bags

into the vestibule,
I trailing behind
without a word.

We were now, I saw,
in the milieu
of very aged women

in the final
stages of disease
and infirmity.

They were walking
slowly,
step by step,

uncertain, hesitant,
to and from
their rooms.

"*Femme je suis,
pauvre et ancienne.*"

My wife of many years
just stood with Shade
and looked on

not knowing what to say,
the *physical* sight
was so overpowering.

For the first time
I was alone
with my fate

and fell inward
to the center
where it was stark

and utter, locked in,
my eyes distraught
and lost.

My body remained
through all this
tall and straight,

however, towering,
it seemed to me,
over the little

white-haired ladies
as if asserting
my eternal distinction.

At that moment
three very frail women,
better dressed

than the others,
appeared, limping
slowly towards me

from the dining room,
absorbed in talking.
I saw only the smaller

of the three. Goodness
like a philosopher's stone
irradiated the air

around her, her demeanor
kind and gentle,
what I imagine as Hebraic,

but in the exquisite
proportion of qualities,
the exquisite reserve,

she was a lady
from a far countree
(probably North)

with delicate white hair.

As she approached,
she looked up
and our eyes met

and I felt good
in her presence.
Walking over,

I greeted her
as a kindred spirit
and with a gallant

but restrained gesture
I bent over
as if to help her.

Smiling softly
she acknowledged this
and walked on.

By God, I thought,
I'm going to make it.
But it was not so.

IV   The Song

A circle of chairs.
Voices of aged ladies
and an Adam.

Outside the circle
a young woman, smiling,
with a guitar.

She greets each by name
as they approach slowly
from the dining room

and settle in their chairs.

In the biblical vapors
kindness, sweetest
of the small notes

in the world's ache,
most modest and gentle
of the elements,

entered man before history
and became his daily
connection, let no man

tell you otherwise.

The playing begins
on tremulous strings.
Heartily she sings

and calls on them
with her eyes,
her urgent being,

to sing along,
she will sustain them.
Her young spirit,

undaunted, pleads
to stay old age,
to disregard all odds

and obliterate it,
calling on song to help,
and faintly one voice

responds and a few heads
nod to the strong beat,
but Adam's eyes are closed

and some have one eye open
and the other X-ed out
as in a cartoon.

When the song is over,
there are little smiles
here and there

and the faces are not
quite so cheerless.
Slowly then the ladies

stand up and disband,
lumbering by as before.
When he saw me, Adam

stopped a moment
with a friendly look
as if glad to find

a man to chat with,
but he's had a stroke
and is now forever

about to speak.

Another time, another singer,
of majestic girth under
Calpurnia's headpiece,

looking straight ahead
into the space
of Handel and opera

as she pleaded with Caesar
not to go to the Senate
that day (never mind that

after the event she moved
his money and papers
to Anthony's house...

we have Plutarch's
word for it).
In any case,

the style was the thing,
full-bosomed, heroic,
industrial age or no.

God, how she sang,
very erect under
her crow's nest,

leaning back slightly,
defying all modern modes,
and the small hairs

on my back tingled
and I felt cold
inside and faint.

Wife, if music be
the conduit of death,
play on!

V   Who

Word now came,
my room was ready.
A nurse led us

down a long hallway
and my wife and Shade,
the executioners,

followed with my bags
to a clean room
of exact arrangement:

two identical blond dressers,
two plain beds,
two identical armchairs,

slightly worn,
the scene blanched
of former occupants.

My wife busied herself
and hung my favorite
landscape over the bed

and set an old snapshot
on the mantle
to remind me who I was.

I could see a younger man
there and a woman, smiling
and in vigorous health

whose excess radiated
from them in tiny pulses.
I could see

but not remember.

On the other dresser
a similar snapshot.
Of the absent room-mate.

In the picture he is
standing in the sun
in shirt-sleeves,

an ordinary man,
middle-aged,
being photographed.

Next to him,
also in shirt-sleeves,
David Ben Gurion,

the prime minister
equally plain.
No other sign

of the room-mate.
Being led down the hall
by a nurse, no doubt.

Parting was not hard
for me that day
since my wife was coming back

the next morning, which
she did and took me for
a drive in the park

and we walked
in the spring flowers.

And the head nurse,
a bluff, good-natured
black woman came by

my room and introduced
herself by her first name.
I liked her at once

and gave her mine.
And after the paper
ran a story on me

I danced with the dark-eyed
singer who came on Fridays
and had a tender visit

with my brother,
as when we were boys.
But I could not hold on.

I ate well, yet became
gaunt and agitated
and could no longer be

trusted in the dining room
and had to have
my meals brought to me.

My absent room-mate
had come back,
a small harmless old man

but incontinent. I paid
no attention to him
except to his stench

at which I raged
and shouted.
And I expostulated

with my wife: "We've been
together fifty years.
Why do I have to be here?

Aren't we husband and wife?"
Then my memory got worse.
I was now no longer able

to read, or to write my name
but only my wife knew.
God, how restless I was!

and menaced! I had to escape.
But I was afraid
I would be stopped

and questioned
at the front door.
At siesta time,

therefore, I climbed
over a wall and
wandered for hours through

black neighborhoods,

lost!

How can I
explain my confusion?
Women had to bathe

and dress me now,
overworked grandmothers,
poor, black,

whom in former years
I would have hailed
compassionately

but I was terrified
and raised my fist
when they approached.

"What's the matter?
Don't you trust us?"
said the head nurse,

the voice sure, steady.
I couldn't answer.
"Don't you trust *me*?"

"I trust you."
Nevertheless they
were terrifying

and I struck back
and had to be strapped
to my chair.

God knows what
my medications were!
Then my kidneys failed.

I was rushed to a hospital
and had only a few days
to live but I survived.

The question now was,
How much longer?
The Home would not

take me back and I was
transferred, therefore,
to a locked facility

where I died in a coma
on a Saturday evening,
September 9th, whether

from Alzheimer's or
another kidney failure
or because I had not

pissed in nine days
I do not know,
but thus I ended

who had upheld the
poetic impulse and
looked on with dismay

at its undoing by
innumerable theorists.

Coda

"God, if I had
known I was
going to live

to 97, I would
have took better
care of myself."

No response.

The giber's
crucified himself.

Where's Parakletos?

In a ballad.

Ambiguous reader,
should I have been
more devious?
more intellectual?

The compassionate
Shade stood silent
in my integrity,
looking eternal.

"He is my adversary!"
"Adieu," he muttered
and dissolved.

What country is this?

of old words
an old country

country:
      ding! dong!

old heart
old God

steorfan

MEDITATIONS

MEDITATION I

In the dead of night
the caribou slept.

The possibility of not knowing
what you are
had not yet been conceived.

It is the original forest.
There is peace.

The wolf has eaten.
He goes into a long howl
to give his location.

If the hunter does not find him,
he'll live seven years.

A box is a box.
Integrity has been defined.

MEDITATION II

Atomic man streamed
into the cosmos
on a mathematical formula.

Poetic man streamed
into destiny on a book.

What is the question?

The mind answered
with a category

but intuito, the maestro
of the absolute,

and signore serio, the heart
answered silently.

HELLO

Early man
faces
the Unknown

looks at it
smells it
feels it

rubs it
shakes it
listens:

Ah,
the divine
scientist!

MEDITATION III

There never was
a simple world

since Adam,
nor a kind one

with a fanfare
to the common man

yet there's music
in the lot
of the Adamite.

History, blow, blow.
Fiddle this:

who spits
in the glass

eye of Moloch?
nobody, nobody

MAN AT WORK

Every other man
runs a business.
Every fourth man
is professional.

A table
not with four legs
but with statistical legs.

This is that strangest
of all worlds, *numbers*,
which no one can enter
as a whole man
nor leave behind

for it is the principle
of the mind at work
its style, its strict
proportions
its alignment
its very faculty

that timeless order
which is bilk to poets,
wholly without heart or humor,
immaterial as fairy
yet the frame of industry

the grub of scholars
the final sawdust
of the absolute.

124

MEDITATION IV

Heavy hangs
          the age of occupation
over the romantic head.

Who will now be greater
          than the sabre-toothed tiger
and preserve the divine proportion
          of a game of chess?

Who will sit
          in his mind
and scan
          the planet
as a small island?

Who will remember
          that when Osiris
is at 12
          on the dial
and the invention
          of surveying
is at 6,
          it's Egypt?

Who will be left
          to smell
the pine
          and eucalpytus
and make
          a theme-head
impersonate a god?

MEDITATION V

Lord, what is man?
                    He looks into a glass
and sees a physical figure
                            looking back at him,
the two waiting immobile
                          for him to reappear
as the world knows him,
                         by name, by work, by habits,
in what particulars
                 he is significant,
and... why should it be embarrassing
                            to speak of this?
... in what endearing...
                    Is he honest?
and how he looks
               when meditating...
all in a semblance characteristic
                      as his bones,
including that shade
               in the inwit of presence,
his secondary at the subliminal portal,
that stands for more
                 potentiality than appears,
the quiet continent
               behind it feeling boundless
(the worse for him).

The final scene, the only scene,
                      inherent in glass,
is that looker
            waiting for it to happen
and caught in the act.

126

MEDITATION VI

"If you open the brain
    from whence sprang
    Solomon and Aristotle,"
I read,
    "and separate the lips
    in the fissure of Sylvius,
    a triangle of cortex

    will appear.
                This is
    the Island of Reil."

Well put, anatomist.
We are all careful,
men of earth.

Thus Newton pondered
on falling apples
and a blind man
sensed a post.

    "How happy I was,"
wrote the scientist
after a long illness,

    "when once again
    I had something
    to investigate."

MEDITATION VII

What is it that stalks
the intellect
like a Tasmanian devil,

insatiable,
craving to be great?

On the gentle planet
of the soul
where melody

and monologue
accompany the elements
on the way

to philosophy
and the earth,
as when Marilyn plants a bush

and feels the soil
between her fingers,
I meditate:

welcome to the old sod,
welcome!

Cellist, play
those deep notes!

AIE!

There's the greenwood fern
and the open woods
and the smell of hay
and the eye of a frog
and a fern signature
left in a coal

and there is fern
by analogy,
a most ancient weed.

MAN CONTEMPLATING A ROCK

Incipit
>   the first
philosopher
>   & *ad*
infinitum.

MEDITATION VIII

"What are animals for?"

How base the answer
                     must be!
The true north
              of my nature
lies in
        the question.
The sublime
            too, yet it was
only a chance
              association of words,
as when the
            mountains at night
are coupled
            with the image
of Borges
          poring over ancient
documents
          for the language
of mystery.
            Implausible
but in this
            strange genus they
belong together.

THE GLIMMER

a wine shop
a church

between them
an ilex

the minimal village

the philosopher wonders

a quiddity
in the eye?

the eye
in quiddity?

who's that fleeing?

Ah, quiddity!

GENESIS

I

*IN THE BEGINNING
THERE WAS PROTOPLASM*

When I read this in
the morning paper
I was in Genesis at once.

And on another page,
news of a microbe,
Bacillus Inferno,
slowly moving two miles
under ground in rock,
on a diet of iron,
locked in without oxygen
for a 100,000,000 years.

We have been through wars
and old civilizations
but this beats all.

What can outlast them?
physics? calculus?

II   The Dream

After that
I had a dream.

I was in an open space
like an endless loft.
It was empty, yet
I could sense
presences near me.

Were they clones,
electronic in nature?

Then the scene cleared
and I understood
that my fate from now on
was to be here
without human company,
inert, spell-bound.

Then I heard
the soft click
of a switch,
then silence again,
a breathless suspension.

III   The Awakening

I was awakened
by the sound
of a viola from
an open window

and my soul returned
in the deep timbre.

My sex, too,
for in the middle
register the figure of
a heavy, earthy woman
in bare feet appeared.

IV   The Old Sparrow

It was morning
and my paper
was waiting for me.

Scientists in Grenoble
had built a working model
of the early universe

and in Cleveland
they had succeeded
in making chromosomes.

Poets were crying:
"We are losing the earth!"

and an unnamed source quoted
the senator from Alabama
as saying, without so much as
"*Will the gentleman yield?*"

"Go write an ode to the inexorable!"

Men were hurrying to work.
The great corporations
had gone faceless,
and there was panic.

All were moving
through man's time

at a glacial speed,
the alienated,
the despairing.

And philosophers were
mulling over the question:
What is meaning?

My apple tree
was still there.

From my window
I could see its
gnarled, tough bark.

Like Kruschev,
I'm an old sparrow.

You can't muddle me
with your cries.

Note: The last three lines are a quote from Kruschev when he
was visiting the U.S. in his capacity as the Soviet premier and
was heckled during a dinner speech.

A DREAM

Psychologist,
             my mental spider,
hero of time,
              what do you make of this?
"Six days sailing
              north of Britain,"
wrote the unknown
                 sailor
circa 150 A.D.
                  "lies the Utmost Island
of the Sullen Sea."

In such a sea,
             solus,
I lay at zero,
             plumb,
with no way back
                . . . the dream
had not quite passed
                (like an
early Greek hero
             of obscure origin).
There was still
             an instant
image from it
             of deserted streets
and dust and paper
              flying around,
by which I knew
             that the end was approaching
though no way out
             appeared yet from

that turbulent night
                        of continual alarums
in which the human race
                                came out of the ocean
in frightful import,
                    that Passion
staggering to imagine
                        in its ordeal,
and passed through time
                        before my eyes,
I swear it,
              I meanwhile unreal
as in a fever.

No sooner thought,
                    then it was image
and like a great wave
                      broke
and lapped at the shore.

After which these words
                        from the stern,
underlying order
                  of things
were spoken
              in my head,
not loud
              but with a heavy
stress
            in the mouth,
exact and absolute
                      as a stone engraving:
"Pursuant to the Rocks,
                    Thorns!"

I could make nothing
                    of this but poetry
but the utterance was darker
                         and impregnable,
not to be looked at closely
                    nor transcribed
by a stylus on the scale
                    of a lens in
a butterfly's eye.
                    It was meant
to guide me,
            of that I was sure.

That is how I came
                    to know
how God spoke with Moses.

MEDITATION IN A NOTEBOOK

*Insects have
no ears
in their heads*

*The real life
of a telephone
is blank*

Cut it out,
jokester!

*The pupil
of a cat's eye
is vertical*

*A human skeleton
weighs
ten pounds*

Wait a minute!
I've lost
my way. . .

where are we?

*In a bolero.
The Composer
has forgotten*

*to write
        an ending.*

MEDITATION IX

What can be compared to
                        the living eye?
Its East
        is flowering
honeysuckle
                and its North
dogwood bushes.

What can be compared
                    to light
in which leaves darken
                        after rain,
fierce green?
                like Rousseau's jungle:
any minute
            the tiger head
will poke through
                    the foliage
peering
        at experience.

Who is like man
                sitting in the cell
of referents,
            whose eye
has never seen
                a jungle,
yet looks in?

It is the great eye,
                source of security.
Praised be thou,
                as the Jews say,
who have engraved
                clarity
and delivered us
                to the mind
where you must reign
                severe
as quiddity of bone
                forever
and ever without
                bias or mercy,
attrition or mystery.

FIELD NOTES

The sun, known by its metaphor
as a heavenly body,
rose at 7:10 today

and man was in his lingual cage,
pondering, as usual,

and the industrials fell 40 points.

Suddenly, as at the crack of a pistol shot,
the pigeons roosting under the eaves
at Saint Cecilia's flew out in formation

and the city began to stir
in a cubism of tense, set faces,
vendors, panhandlers, street musicians,
the poor as numerous as sparrows.

And the portrait of the banker,
John Julius Augerstein,
hangs in the Courtauld,
self-assured, Olympian,
the steely eyes surprisingly blue.

They glitter, unrelenting, hard,
piercing the viewer
as if he were a small animal.

The portrait has found him out.

And the philosopher ponders,
as the resin on the pine tree
hardens into amber,
                              what is man?

And paints himself
                    into the portrait.

And the poet's in a bibulous mood,
painting himself into a Shakespearian discourse
with a rock three hundred million years old,
baffled by its ancient silence.

> "Come, emit!
> Not even a sigh?
>
> God has damned thee
> with silence
> and us with leaders.
>
> Get me a sculptor
> to work on this.
>
> I know thy physiognomy
> but not thy nature.
>
> How shall I address thee?
> Thou would'st think I am a fool,
> yet I must talk to thee.
>
> Art thou the rock which quidnunc
> sat on, seeking a quietus?
>
> I wonder thou does't not defy
> yet would crumble rather than submit."

Softly now, softly!
The poet's grappling with an invisible self,
a mysterium accompanied by a klavier.

Malaise creeps up on him
like a subtle vapor
and departs as soundless
as it came, incommunicado.

HOW TO BE WITH A ROCK

The explicit ends here.
                              Outer is inner.
It is all manifest.
                      Its character is durity.
There lies its charisma.

By nature it is Pangaea.
                              It has its own face
and its own tomb,
                      the way it stands,
unmoved by destiny,
                      a model for the mind.
We can only be spectators.
                              All is day within.

"Go to the village,"
                      tell my wife,
"and bring back a chicken,
                      an onion, a goose
and an apple
              and we'll lie here
and repopulate this Siberia."

It is in Genesis.
A strange god,
              all torso
and without invention or audacity.

It can be accused of both plutonism
and the obvious.
                      The closest human thing to it

is the novocained tooth,
                    its Medusa hair now fossilized.

It can be bequeathed to one's heirs
with the assurance that it will not depreciate
or be found irrelevant.

MEDITATION X

What rides the galaxies
                          on calculations,
is disinterested as air
                          and long as equanimity,
yet weeps unknowing
                          when it stops,
and shivers,
                withdrawing
like the overbreeding muskrat
                              downcast
at itself?

MEDITATION XI

If it takes almost a million years
                        for light from Andromeda
to reach a learned society

and stars sometimes explode
                        on the astronomer's time scale

and in another hundred million years
                        we shall be able to see
Maffei I, described as "a nearby
                        island universe,"

then there is passion
                        in the lightness of a feather,
man can hear
                        his arteries hardening
and the realist must pass
                        first through the eye of abstraction.

Yet they say it is so.

"A STATELIER PYRAMIS TO HER I'LL REAR THAN RHODOPE'S OF MEMPHIS EVER WAS."

Not in Tennessee

nor in ancient Egypt

but where time

and place shift

as when a dream

draws to its exigent,

there you will see

the real Memphis

radioactive rising

out of memory

with all its pyramises.

150

MEDITATION XII

There is clay, lime, silicon and salt
for the rationalist
                    and something
with a strange atomic weight.

Let Prospero whose I
                    is on a dandelion seed
give it a name
                    to disappear into
as softly
          as a spider hurls a thread
and make it impervious
                    to theory

for although he is fanciful,
                    he loves
salt and iron,
and absolutes make him belch.

MEDITATION XIII

In what sense
         I am I
a minor observer
         as in a dream
absorbed in the interior,

a beardless youth
         unaccountably
remote yet present
         at the action

reminding me faintly
         of Prufrock,
a diminutive figure
         barely discernible
seemingly ageless
         escapes me.

The original impulse
         to sing
compressed
         into one exultant note
breaks out
         of the chest-space,
vibrating along
         the shoulders
in the presence
         of full-bodied
womanliness,
         the eyes dark
in the inner scene,
         the hair long
and black,

       our dark lady,
inmate of courtship.
She does not speak.
          She is nameless.
The reason for her
          presence there
is unknown.

A shepherd,
       vaguely associated,
stands
   at a distance
under
   a birch tree,
causally,
    playing a flute.
Sweetness
    streams across,
also
   from the balance
and the position
     of each
it issues.

Neither moves.
     The scene
is not matter
    that can pall
or diminish.
    Its secret holds
as fast as I.

As in Giorgione
    the suspense
is eternal.

MEDITATION XIV

A man is fiddling with his matchbox
while he talks,
exactly as I saw him
thirty years ago.
I have his tweed coat on
(I can feel the coarse fabric),
his domestic habits,
the abstract look in his eyes.

Now to break out
                    of this straightjacket!

MEDITATION XV

O ancient image,
                    by what strange power
you bind me
                    to the light
of a small
                    metaphysical lamp,
to the light
                    of the swarming city,
and restore
                    my ancient relation
to words,
                    in which I have set
my hope,
                    those that are born
magistrates
                    or old oak,
a test
                    of attention and integrity,
or incline
                    to contemplation,
those that
                    are virtuous
like Medusa
                    in their heads
and some
                    in their bleeding,
and those that
                    are simplest
like *horse* and
                    plow
and remain
                    incorruptible.

We have a pact.
                Nevertheless infinity drones.
Leave me for a while.
                I'll go with Erasmus the Labrador
to his favorite tree
                to sniff for gonads.

"Anyone I know?
                That crazy Afghan again,
the one I romped with.

Mmmm, lamb bone!

Trot home now,
                family waiting."

Lights out.
                Retired, all.

Around and around
                three times
he follows his tail,
                then lowers himself
and sighs and curls up
                at the center,
the day's work done.
                Has licked man's face
and falls asleep
                under his foot,
the loyal eyes
                closed.

Now where,
                ancient spirit?

To a potato patch,

          once the lot of man

when it was said,

      "a clean bowel,
      a clean head",

to cockleburr

      and wild hemp

of the fields.

    There, distant, a

black Angus,

      restorer, restorer

of the ancient

      relation

in whose presence

        man

again is steady,

        single.

I WAS LISTENING TO JEAN REDPATH

sing an old
Scottish ballad

and using the old
form asked myself,

"What is piercing as a horn
and what is quicker than a thorn?

and what is harder than a rock
and what is tighter than a lock?

and what is longer than the way
and what is deeper than the sea?"

"Oh, aspiration's piercing as a horn
and envy's quicker than a thorn,

self-interest's harder than a rock,
defense is tighter than a lock,

abstraction's longer than the way
and man's contemplation of man is

deeper than the sea."

MEDITATION XVI

Where does
justice
hang out?

*Try
the internal
citizen.*

And what
will hold
back rage?

*The pink-white
blossoms of
the apple tree.*

What is
this state
of being?

A pity,

a pity

a pity.

NO ONE TALKS ABOUT THIS

They go in different ways.
One hog is stationed at the far end
of the pen to decoy the others,
the hammer knocks the cow
                            to his knees,
the sheep goes gentle
                        and unsuspecting.
Then the chain is locked
around the hind leg
and the floor descends
                        from under them.
Head down they hang.
The great drum turns
the helpless objects
and conveys them slowly
to the butcher waiting
at his station.
The sheep is stabbed
behind the ear.

Gentle sheep, I am powerless
to mitigate your sorrow.
Men no longer weep
                        by the rivers of Babylon
but I will speak for you.
If I forget you, may my eyes
lose their Jerusalem.

ISRAEL

I hear the voice
            of David and Bathsheba
and the judgment
            on the continual
backslidings
            of the Kings of Israel.

I have stumbled
            on the ancient voice
of honesty
            and tremble
at the voice
            of my people.

BALLAD OF THE DIMINISHED I

Tell me, where does fancy breed?

In the calyx of the crocus
in the springtime, a merry time
when the spirit bounds like a feather.

And a goatherd, two miles out of Oaxaca,
with his flock browsing ahead of him,
approached me and hesitantly,
as a simple man with one more learned,
asked: "What's it like, Señor, in the city?"

And tell me, where does fancy lie?

In a bright star in a Miro.

And how close can we get to quiddity?

As close as a metaphor.

But the jaunty sparrow
skipping around and pecking for seeds
in my garden is its own quiddity,
for does he not sing
when all else cringes?

And compassion, where does it lie?

In a book. O noble book!

And I heard a voice,
"It's sad but let me console thee,
there's always beauty."

And when shall we be safe?

When the crocodile weds with the dove.

And when will fancy die?

When every man is master of his time.

And the design of the universe?
the nature of man?

Pending.

MELANCHOLY

bachelor of music,
                    cum laude,
my shadowy lutenist
                    plucking
nightshade;
            my double
(with the pulse
                of a quiet man)
in residence
            on the left
side of my soul,
                with whom the right side rests
like two pans of a scale
                    at 0;
who radiates
            undiminishing in an own phoenix;
have you not put me,
                my sweet drone,
my genius,
            in touch with Abraham
of my long line?

To borrow the words
                of Isaak Walton
when he wrote
                of the nightingale,
"Lord, what music hast thou
    provided for the saints in heaven!"

MEDITATION XVII

reverence,
            His great
shadow
            is in the word.
I tremble.
            He has sent
a messenger
            in the slow
grave measures
                    of music.
Yet I know
            not what
to revere.

"MARCIA FUNEBRE"

When I see those words,
I hear the timbre
of a deep music,
and my heart leaps,
my pulse quickens,
and I am in my
                    true
habitat.

But when I come
                    to meaning,
I crave
        I whimper

Where is the music
                of my soul?

Uneasy stand-off.
Only the theologian
ventures to answer.

MEDITATION XVIII

the cock crows
the ant rushes
the bird sings:
my turf, my turf, my turf

the soul asks,
what's who?
and disappears
into its nature

where is eternity?

in lingua oscura

the cock crows
the ant rushes

MEDITATION XIX

The widower
              lies under
a stone
              anon

sans eyes
              sans code
sans I
       the observer

with a
      damned subject.

Alas,
       metaphysician.

MEDITATION XX

If one could write
               like St. Augustine,
not for an inner audience,
                    or readers,
but for God,
            there would always be
an honest accounting
               from that depth
where, out of compassion,
                  the curtain was drawn
on the body's terrible
              import until it fell
unloved
        into its final disease
and the tortured
            irreversible meaning
entered the sick cell,
             where none play games.

I know this
           yet am still intimidated
by the prospect
            of an audience,
to which I play,
           though this be ectoplasm
to a sage.

NOCTURNE

Death, have you
no meaning?

Is meaning foreign
to the universe...

a mere construct,
as in mathematics?

Oh death, is this
thy nocturne?

THE RESPONSE TO HAMLET

Leakey
        holding
the skull
        of Zinjanthropus,
1,500,000 years
            in his hand.

NUCLEAR ODE

We shall all lie in the sun
                            and bask.

You too, hunter.
There shall be no more loners,
                            do you hear?

THE AGE

I shall
       not prevail.
The heart
       is my negritude.

SATYRICON

THE WASHINGTON SCENE

Anno Domini

Lucifer's
      at his lute again.

Merde!

EYE, WHAT DO YOU SEE?

THE DOW JONES INDUSTRIAL
AVERAGE ROSE FOUR POINTS

BONDS SLIPPED (LINGERING
INFLATION WORRIES)

Where am I?

There goes my soul
                    down the street.

Hey, wait!

No, it's my sense of self
whose eye is my imperium.

Imperium speaks:

TECHNOLOGY AND RETAIL SALES
LED A LATE RECOVERY
THE MARKET IS OPTIMISTIC

Be serious!

At that my soul spoke:
    All that is left is irony
    which is best served like Chardonnay
    with cold crab and grilled words.

SATYRICON

Guess what? Little pygmies
from the business world
have taken over Congress

with a mission to scuttle
social welfare, their ancient enemy.

Incroyable! Who are they?

Wait, here comes one.
Let's ask him,

"Sir, who are you?"

"I was born in a log cabin..."

"That's enough!"

Here's another.

"Sir, could you tell us
who you are?"

"Excuse me, but I'm late,
I'm on my way to the presidency."

Let's ask an ordinary citizen.

"Sir, how do you feel about this?"

"I feel like Prometheus
chained to a limitless
and bare universe

held together by rigor
and the same old working man,
his nose to the grindstone,

while investors and billionaires
swarm in the city."

As on a distant planet
devoid of public events
a beggar stands

most patiently
with a tin cup,
an engraving for the ages.

THE ACTORS

Maxwell a corporation head
a self-made man
who loves his creator

Strangelove a fundamentalist
who has the total clarity
of a small mind

Luger a talk-show host
a curious mixture
of geniality and venom

Meriwether a Socialist.
Had he lived
when the world was created

he would have offered
the creator
some valuable suggestions

Primrose an optimist
who instinctively
lives on ambrosia

and leaves everything
he can't digest
on his plate

Dulcimer a celebrated
poet a sheep
in sheep's clothing

Pixel a modest
little man
of few words.

Curtain!

the play is beginning:
A Comedy of Errors.

SARCASMUS

Young utopia of spring
                    greens,
hello,
        light up the towers
of the Whisky King,
behold the mints
and comics of the season
as the tempers light our reason
with penumbra and with chroma.

The Pollys in the Tenderloin
size up the town and vocalize.
The wise guy plucks a banjo string
for Polly's Irish eyes.

Only the fathers of the state
have public welfare up their sleeves.

Big-hearted Dick obeys the law
and trots around in chevron weaves
with dividends from anchored markets,
picking his manner from the facts

of God, the flying American.

THE LAST ACT OF A SARDONIC PLAY

The playwright is thinking:
"Here's to man
  at the head of his table.
  Long life to him,
  a man of slime, a rat-trap,
  but a god at words."

YES

So much
depends

upon the
instant

wrist
watch

on the
executive

a thyroid
pill

a clean
bowel

CHARACTERS

I   Romeo and Juliet

Yeah, I know her.

               Comes from this neighborhood.

Guys go bananas

          when they see her

the way bees

        zero in

on quince blossoms:

Puss, puss,

         the forbidden female:

never get enough of that;

               sell their own mothers

(they think) to dive

           into the puss of voluptas.

But let me tell you,

         she's bad news.

Breaks balls!

II   Schneider Agonistes

"Look!"

He held up his right fist

locked around a steel ball.

Then as he turned, a gloating
held the face,
                    and in the eyes
a glimmer as if looking inward
at distinction. . . and held on.

"I was in the hospital.
I didn't want you to know."

Let all see.
                    Considerate.
Pity standing by.

"They cut me open from this ear"

Compassion wrestling with a capon

"down along the jugular to scrape
the carotids."
                    Ah, greatness!

Schneider, you who have never uttered
one memorable word,
                    as scoff is my witness,
le coeur oblige
                    that I bestow on you
cockleburr for your obscurity,
one for each year,
and the Order of Iron for your suffering.

III   The Psychologist

Great Lucifer begat him

                 with many voices

(they get around...

             ask Gilgamesh).

Was he put on earth

          to discover light?

Off he dashes, subtle,

             self-conscious,

to probe heaven itself.

           Brash bugger!

IV   Poem Beginning *JEW*

He filled his glass to the brim
and lifted it as if to toast me
but instead called me by name :

             "RAKOSI!"

He put the accent on the first syllable.
It rang out like a command.
Had he been drinking?

"RAKOSI!" he snapped,
"You come from an ancient tribe.
  Put the night into words for me."

  Another time, another voice:
"I know thee.
  I am of thy tribe.
  I know thy sickness."

  Was he serious?
  Was I his wise old Jew?
  the serious Jew?
  I thought we were friends.

  Put the night into words!
  the night of small creatures,
  of Bartok's night quartets?

  Easier to put death into words,
  the ultimate which makes one kind
  and puts the warthog on alert.

  This old Jew is simple, you can quote him:
"How beautiful the night is!
  I think I'll take a stroll in the woods."

SHAKESPEARIAN STREET

Here comes one
who sits
in high places

and would skin
a flea for the
hide and fat,

an entrepreneur.
Stay clear or
you'll wind up

in his pocket.
And here's one
equally adversarial

who sits in his
skin above reality
nuancing words

and looking as if he
had an empyrean
in his pocket

and would not trade
his metaphors for
all the cash

in China, a poet,
the original
crêpe-hanger.

TO THE MAN INSIDE

"A woman's heart is like an inn"
Russian saying

Get up, you old dog.
You've been lying in front
of the fire too long.

Out! Out! The inn
is temporarily closed
for remodelling.

The ladies are inside
cleaning house and laughing
at the inn idea.

"Say, boss," minces
one, "who's
the inkeeper here?"

The new tenant
is indistinct.

Will there be larks
and metaphors
at the inn, sweet ladies?

THE BLACK SLAVE

as Stepin Fetchit might have written it

It's true, master.
Ah never liked to work.
Even sittin on my ass
was too much for me.

But master's in the cold
cold ground and ah'm
sittin here, laughin.

Note: Stepin Fetchit was a black movie actor who used to parody the stereotype of the negro as lazy and witless and make people laugh without their knowing just why they were laughing.

MODERN NARRATIVE

In the Old Testament
I sat by the waters
of Babylon and wept

and I sat with a simple
shoemaker's son,
Thomas Traherne and wept

as he was meditating:
'I learned all the dirty
devices of the world.'

Now corporate man sits
by the waters of time,
studying his odds.

GRAVEDIGGERS

Look at this headstone

Joe Anders
b. Nov. 6, 1903   d. Sept. 12, 1989

A MAN OF UNSWERVING INTEGRITY

This guy must have come from
The Home For Comedians

For once I'd like to see one
that reads
Here lies Joe Anders
I do hereby declare
As God Is My Witness
That I Was An Ordinary Fellow
Inoffensive
With All My Cash In Bonds

Amen!

Let's bury this poor bastard now.
Another one will come along soon.

THE ORDEAL OF MOSES

In 1508 Michael Angelo made a silverpoint drawing of his patron, Pope Julius II. It showed only a few scraggly hairs on top. In 1509 the drawing became Zacharias on the ceiling of the Sistine Chapel. The beard now was long and white, the head was all bald. This Julius looked Syrian or Greek. Not long afterward he reappeared as a statue on his own tomb. This time he was called Moses.

Moses? A pope! Nephew of Sixtus IV, formerly bishop of Capentras, Archbishop of Avignon, Cardinal-priest of S. Pietro-in-Vincoli, Cardinal-Bishop of Sabina, etc, etc.? *This* pope had been educated by the Franciscans and had sent out missionaries to convert three continents. What could Michael Angelo have been thinking of?

Of course, in a way, he was paying a great compliment to the Jews, although to the Renaissance artist, Moses had probably become just Man with a capital M. One can imagine Michael Angelo searching all through history and concluding that the one name that would immortalize his dead friend among all men was Moses. In using that name he was proclaiming to posterity that Julius II too had been close to God and stood out like Moses, the supreme lawgiver.

To the Jews, of course, this is not an innocent matter. Compliments are all right but Jews are wary of being ingested by them. They much prefer Moses to remain exactly as the Gentiles found him. You can't blame them for being suspicious, any more than you can blame Christians for wanting to get in on the divine action.

There is always the possibility, of course, that the artist had simply run out of titles. Anyhow, if you look at his figure, you will see that this man could never have been Moses. Or a pope either. The bearing is heroic. He is a seated Neptune, all body, with epic limbs and a long beard swirling and overflowing his lap. Two horns representing rays of light protrude from the forehead. A cloth is draped loosely across the knees, as on antique statues of barbarians. Only the left foot looks humble and tired, as if it might have trudged up Mt. Sinai. This lapse, I concluded, must have occurred when the artist allowed his attention to wander. Perhaps by that time he himself was tired.

Thackeray's opinion of this Moses was, "I would not like to be left alone in a room with it!" My own opinion is that such a Jew is yet to be born. If he were to appear, he'd make a sensation. After all, there's nothing mythical about Jews.

In my synagogue, however, this is not known. There in a dimly lit corridor leading to a door marked MEN, above a glass case displaying the great horn of God, a magnificent long, twisted ram's horn, and an ancient shield of torah, whose commandments come straight from Moses himself, stands a two-foot high bronze replica of this barbarian god who was once Pope Julius II. It rests on a discreet walnut base and has a bronze plaque fastened by two small screws, also bronze and discreet: In Memory of Lt. Sidney Abrams by His Parents.

By rights I should say something about this to somebody but it's pretty late in the day to do anything. No one remembers Lt. Abrams or his family any more or even knows in which war he lost his life, but I still wouldn't want to offend his memory or the friends of the family who must have congratulated themselves on the selection. What better memorial to a lost son than a figure of Moses by one of the greatest artists of all time?

As for the rabbi, I wouldn't want to trouble him with another problem. He's a nice guy. He has more than he can keep up with already. Besides, I suspect that I couldn't get anywhere with the problem anyhow. I can hear the objections now:

"What difference does it make? Who's going to stop to examine a statue on his way to the Men's Room?"

"It's the intention that counts, the sentiment."

"What statue? I never saw a statue there."

"If what you say is true, it will help the Jews. It can't but enhance the image for people to know that a great gentile like that conceived of one of us on such a grand scale."

"He must have been inspired at least a little by our example. That's worth something, isn't it? Furthermore, if we revere learning, how can we reject a grand conception, even if it isn't altogether Jewish? Besides, you said the left foot might have been on Sinai."

The Chairman of the Arts Committee had been waiting to get her anger under control. The strain showed in her tight lips and cold eyes and in her extraordinary politeness.

"I know a little something about art. A great artist takes great liberties. There's a deeper meaning there that you're not seeing because you're looking at the work from a narrow view."

Then looking beyond me and addressing enlightened mankind, she finished me off:

"I never know what's meant when people say that a work of art is *Jewish*. Do you?"

MY EXPERIENCES IN PARNASSUS

A Modern Satire

I first started writing when I discovered its extraordinary opportunities for concealment. If anybody had told me that someday I would be attracted by concealment, I would have been deeply offended and indignant. Nothing could have been further from my understanding of myself.

My parents were quite open, straightforward people, a bit heavy-handed but without guile. Their word was clear and dependable. There was never any trouble knowing exactly what they meant. On questions of social justice my father was a pillar of idealism. I loved him for that, but I had seen enough, even as a child, to know that the world was not at all idealistic. Hence there was something not quite right about his idealism. These doubts disappeared, however, when I began to read Tolstoy and Dickens, and since in my dealings with people I was always honest, I continued to think of myself as open and guileless.

My first exposure to concealment was in a writing class in college. I was writing my heart out in my usual straightforward way on what I thought was the wavelength of poetry, but no matter how hard I tried, I could never get better than a "B" on a poem. The only one who got A's was a Japanese student. When I examined his poems, my heart sank and I broke into a sweat. His were the real thing!

There was no particular meaning in his poems. In fact, it was impossible to say what they were really about. They had a few images, quite simple, none particularly compelling, but they had an ambience far beyond their aggregate. I studied this ambience diligently but I was unable to crack its secret code. Its language was sparse and a bit hazy—he couldn't have had more than a couple of hundred English words in his vocabulary—and yet altogether sufficient. There was no denying it, he was a born master of deception. I was deeply shaken by this confrontation and felt miserable. What would become of me now?

Fortunately, before long, I discovered modern French poetry. This poetry instantly put me into a hypnotic state in which I did not know what was happening. All I could see was a strange richness, yet nothing was being said. I could interpret this in only one way: by some manipulation of concealment a rich, bewitching effect was being induced. That was an eye-opener. Obviously, to do this took guile. But guile for what purpose? Certainly not to improve anything. How could you do that by concealing?

This forced me to examine the nature of this guile more closely. In doing so, I perceived that poetry had components built in which lent themselves to guile. The voice, for example. Where did *it* come from? The author hadn't thought of something to say, then used his normal voice to say it. He wouldn't get far doing that. No, the voice was not one that his wife and children would ever recognize as his. Whose then was it? And to whom was it speaking? Not to an audience. There was no audience yet. And even if there was not going to be one, the voice would have spoken as it did. This was a mystery.

Not, of course, because of guile. It would be a mystery in any case. But if the voice in a poem was not recognizable, it could be construed that this was because the poet was trying to win adulation for all the eccentricities and excesses of his imagination by passing them off in the voice of a higher power. This shows you how nimble guile is in slipping into inner sanctums. Always on the look-out for an opportunity and the first to spot one and appropriate it for its own use. A mystery, obviously, is always an opportunity. You can do almost anything with it. After all, it's not going to stand up and shout, "Stop! You got me all wrong."

No less mysterious was poetry's other stock component, the image. God only knows where *it* came from! But there it was, all of a sudden, at the precise spot where a moment before, the poet was fumbling around for something, he didn't yet know what. It would not be true to say that this was what he had been looking for. He had not been clear enough in his mind for that. All he knew was that one minute he was fumbling and the next minute, there was the image. To be sure, it was not *exactly* what he had been reaching for. By some unaccountable good fortune, it turned out to be better. This happenstance, however, had to be kept secret if one wanted credit for it.

In any case, now that the image had materialized, there was something tangible for everybody to see. The presumption was that this alluring presence was a representation of what the author had been groping for. Therein lay the guile, for an image is a *sui generis*; yet how strangely satisfying and fulfilling! And how wonderful that one could get credit for it. It was enough to convert a Hottentot to pretense.

Add to this the curious fact that poetry has no audience except other poets. This means that the poet has no responsibility to laymen. He is free to do whatever will most astonish other poets. In other words, there is nothing he may not do. And since it is not so easy to astonish other poets, he comes eventually to the conclusion that there is nothing he *should* not do.

And, in fact, there is very little that he *will* not do, so great is the power of the imagination to invent and to pretend and to enjoy its creations, and so great is the power of words to proliferate, and so accessible the opportunity in poetry for a man to slip in under cover of a persona all of his obsessions and detestations and unaccountable dreads, as well as all those things which he would be ashamed to reveal openly—his need to be admired, yet frank, to be grandiose, his proclivity for being fascinated by his own sexual fantasies, his inexplicable impulse to freak out in feelings of unreality, etc.

I could see all this was being consciously preserved for the benefit of mankind by the readiness of people to take a writer at his word, and that this was not an activity in which humor would be welcome.

Knowing now that I would have to astonish the poets, my next task was to determine to what end all this pretense was being enacted. I could only conlude that its purpose was to put on a performance and that the performance was an end in itself.

How can I describe what a profoundly liberating effect this discovery had on me? In a flash I was purged of exactly the things that had been troubling my poetry and keeping me from getting ahead. It was now perfectly clear that if poetry was expected to be a performance, the lyric impulse was not necessary. There were more spectacular ways to put on a performance. What a relief it was to know that! It is no secret that a man can wait for years for a lyric impulse. To some it never comes. Surely this was more democratic. It made it possible for anyone to be a poet.

Furthermore, if poetry was expected to be a performance, sincerity also was not necessary. It was, after all, only a show. I need not tell you how sticky the matter of sincerity can be. A poet has to be dead sure of who he is and what he knows and stands for and wants, and at the same time be extraordinarily un-self-conscious in order to get just the right tone of sincerity. Now, thank God, I did not have to be concerned with that. Nor with another problem that had stymied me: what I wanted my imagination to do with reality. For the first time I was free from these burdens, free to turn my whole attention to the art of writing.

With these bits of insight firmly in my grasp, and free of the encumbrances of lyric impulse, reality and sincerity, I took up the problem of how to become famous. This was not as difficult as it looked at first, for it became quickly apparent that what I would have to do is write twenty or more volumes of verse. Since I was only twenty when I made this discovery, I would still be young enough at the end of this enterprise to enjoy my fame. I therefore wrote diligently, one volume each year for twenty years. The critics were over-awed. They had to acknowledge that I was a major poet.

Of course this was not the only way to achieve fame. One could also get there by being a hallucinatory paranoiac. That sort of thing seems to have an irresistible fascination for critics. Since hallucinations have a strange power which they are unable to fathom, they have concluded that hallucinations are a sign of genius.

Another possibility would have been to commit suicide. That was a sure way of achieving immortality, but I decided that that would be too strenuous.

There is only one thing more to tell. I found that when I trained my nose to detect which way the wind would be blowing and pointed my imagination in that direction, making sure that I was always standing next to a man of influence, I became known as a leading innovator, the spokesman of the age.

Now that I am a major poet, I no longer suffer from the unrelenting celebrity of my contemporaries. Would I have been able to overcome my mediocrity if I had remained honest? I don't know. All I know is that nothing looks more profound than obscurity and yet is as impenetrable as obsidian. If it was not meant to be used, why is it there?

It may be that you don't have a need to conceal anything in particular but you do have a hankering for style. That's enough to lead you to guile.

In any case, this is how I became a major poet.

POETICS FROM CHELM

There is no higher authority than theory.

*   *   *

Its medium is poetry's best subject-matter.

*   *   *

Substance is no longer decisive. For every poem now there are a dozen exegetes to supply it.

*   *   *

It takes great discipline to be spontaneous.

*   *   *

Poems keep getting smaller and smaller not because they have less to say but because they have become more rigorous.

*   *   *

On the other hand, the more impenetrable a poem is, the greater.

*   *   *

Surrealist poetry can disarm criticism by suggesting that it might be a comedy.

*   *   *

In today's world the only viable reality is to pretend to be playing a game.

* * *

On the other hand, the world we live in is so monstrous that genius now must be measured by its capacity to create commensurate monsters.

* * *

We are the unacknowledged legislators of the world but we mustn't let it go to our heads.

Note: In Yiddish folk humor *Chelm* was a city of half-wits whose absurdities were so preposterous that the listener laughed and instantly felt more kindly towards his own.

HUMORESQUE

For
mortuary
services

call in
the master
poet,

he whose
architecture
makes

death
perfectly
oblivious.

DRÔLES DE JOURNAL (1924 –

AUG. 7, 1972

The other day
        I was typing *Aug. 7, 1972*
and forgot to
        drop to lower case.
Instantly a communication
            appeared
which circulates ordinarily
only among its own kind:
           AUG. &, !(&@.
It had the allure of the impenetrable.
                In fact,
it didn't have to be understood at all,
even on whether it cared for human beings.
That was its greatest charm.
            In short
it was grounded
        on the unconditional,
one of the attributes of beauty.

CONCEPTION

a plankwalk to the sea

a smoked salmon on a line

a ball of packing twine

everything in eggs and cubes

as effortless and helpless
as waiting for a corpse
with Jockey Club and heliotrope

here comes the bride
with kewpie blue eyes
and a lighted brassiere

it's a gay life
for the humorist
with a gardenia
in his lapel

THE VISION

           flashed
across my mind,
               as on a billboard
...jumbo
         ...the letters lit up

SHOOT THE ENGLISH PROFESSOR

I owe somebody
             an explanation
but it's too late.
             I've already laughed.

ON SOME LINES
BY GAEL TURNBULL

'It's the dottiest
village. Nothing
ever happens there.

When a hen lays
an egg, they ring
the church bells.'

There's a local
library the size
of a tool shed

with nothing on
the shelves later than
The Battle of the Marne.

Children are born
three houses
down the street and

people die next door
and yet it always
knocks them sideways.

ODE TO A NIGHTINGALE

Such claims
        for this little bugger,
this "light-winged
        dryad of the trees,"

this romantic.
                Where is it now?

I don't know.
                I've never seen one.
Not common in
        the Middle West.

Maybe off to see
        the Saint Louis Cardinals,
or his broker,

or to attend
        a memorial service
for the demise
        of the simple.

The barber's girl friend,
        Big Ass, walks by.

Some nightingale!

THE EXPERIMENT WITH A RAT

Every time I nudge that spring
                              a bell rings
and a man walks out of a cage
assiduous and sharp
                    like one of us
and brings me cheese.

How did he fall
                into my power?

PUNK ROCK

I have an act, Polonius,
that will twist your tail.
By burning, I become a symbol,
but not seriously...
we have come too late
to be serious...
an act, Polonius,
for killing two birds,
matter & anti-matter,
with one stone, wackery.

wacky   wackhead   wackery

As it lay amort, the voice
of my spirit cried,
                    "Absent thee
from the real brimstone awhile.
Neither serious
                    nor lyrical be."

Hence nothing I do
makes any difference.
But I have an ear
for the Heretical Imperative.

My cockatoo's gone mad.
He's trying out a new
art form: conniption
to the power of X
and genitals as actors,

212

claiming Rimbaud's space
and all its perquisites.
It takes a demon now
to hold Persephone.

A fart.
                And the reply:
"I hear you calling me."

The people can go to hell
The reader can go to hell

O to be a tiger
by the principle thereof!
to stalk the avant garde
the fictive
and still burn bright.

Tiger, tiger,
heartless, modish,
singular.

I've lost Polonius,
my adversary,
and the larks.

IN A BAR

Neon sign
        in front
THE ELECTRIC FETUS
Holds me!

Hippie
        has joined
psychedelic
          cock
with comic
          put-on.

Is no joker
        going to
challenge
        the vinyl
image?

I'm a goner.
          The new age
has me
        in a mickey
speeding
        towards the
telegraphic
        divination
of the ghoul
        of heroin

foreshadowed
        in surrealist
night speech
        on the media,
its first robot.

APPARITION IN A BUS

Man
    in his fifties,
face
    spare, closed,
reading
      TIME.
Protruding
      from the beige
stormcoat...
        French cuffs,
a pear outline,
      light blue.

Abigail
    out of New Bedford,
the wife,
    her watermark,
the fabric
    washed
by her
    (face closed)
like fine lace,
      its immaculate
conception
    ironed
and folded
    with care.
By conservatrix
of the straight way.
Out of the generations
      of man.

In bed
        I imagine
she allows
            passage
(if my sclerotic
                apparition holds)
but not to you,
            O wild ass
of Mongolia!

FRANKFURT AND BETHLEHEM

This postcard has the Christmas
spirit with its Lutheran
steeple between the hills
its cow fence   its fir tree
and a dirt farm in Thuringia

bright star,
unto you is born
this day a grub
               in the addle.

VERY SHORT POEM ON A
RACING FORM

Wouldn't you know it?

           Autobiography

won

           by a nose.

A lot

           of horse there!

THE SENSE OF HISTORY

It is not the roll
                 your own
cigarette paper
                 that is gay
and open
                 and unmistakably
American
                 but the trade-mark

THE ZIGZAG SAILOR

ITEM

Why is a wizard referred to
                    with admiration
and a witch
            as foul?

Look into this,
            O women's
liberation movement!

MAGISTER QUA MAGISTER

Who could not be a judge
if he donned the robe
and uttered maxims?

But would magister
be magister
without his robe?

For that matter,
is a maxim a maxim
without that robe?

Hard to say.
All in the hands
of anonymous.

A MAN OF UNWAVERING INTEGRITY

What are they going to put
on his headstone?

he was inoffensive

an American citizen

Imp, you have bollixed up
my honorable intentions.

THE IRISH BOY

I don't know what's got into that rooster.
First, he appointed himself the morning herald,
now he's out there on the roof proclaiming
to one and all that every hen within sight
belongs to him...his, his, his...
and that he intends to go down to the hen house
and lay them all, none will be spared,
and if anybody wants to take exception to this,
let him come forward and he will personally
take them all on, one by one or in the aggregate;
otherwise, let the sleepers hold their peace.

LETTERS
TO THE WELFARE DEPARTMENT

I

"To whom
 it may concern:
I have no
 children yet
as my husband
 is a truck driver
and works
 day and night."

We understand!

II

"Gentlemen,
          in answer
to your letter
          I have
given birth
          to a ten
pound boy.

I hope
          this is
satis-
          factory."

Zeus himself
          couldn't have
done better!

III

"Dear Welfare,
          this is
my eighth
          child.

What are you
          going to do
about it?"

You will hear
          in due time
from Oceanus!

IV   The Real Penelope

"Madam,
          I am glad
     to report
               that my husband
     who is missing
               is dead!"

V

"As you requested,
        I am forwarding
my marriage
        certificate
and my three
        children,
one of which
        as you can see
is a mistake."

That was
            to be
expected!

VI Dirge

"This is
        to let
you know
        that my husband
got his
        project cut off
two weeks ago
        and I
have not
        had any
relief since."

VII   Ode

"Dear Sirs:
         you have
branded
         my son
illiterate.
         This is
a dirty lie
         as I
was married
         a week
before he
         was born."

A natural
         mistake
under the
         circum-
stances.

230

VIII

"To whom
        it may
concern:
        unless
I get
        a check soon
I will be
        forced
to lead
        an immortal
life."

Threats
        will get you
nowhere!

Envoi

Ladies, forgive me.
This was the work
of the cock-eyed muse.

COUNTRY EPITAPHS

Axel Hendrix, railroad conductor
b. Feb.10, 1860   d. March 31, 1921
PAPA, DID YOU FIND YOUR WATCH?

The widow Fairchild also spoke
                         into a headstone:
AT LAST I KNOW WHERE HE IS AT NIGHT!

The widow Benson was brief,
                         the words chiselled:
GONE BUT NOT FORGIVEN!

And here's a husband's last words
                         to his wife in stone:
SHE WAS BORN TO RULE!

And yonder is a whole novel
                         on a tombstone:
I TOLD YOU I WAS SICK!

And here's a humorist:
                         ON THE WHOLE
I'D RATHER BE IN PHILADELPHIA!
Ha!

Hello, what's this? under a crucifix!
THEY DON'T MAKE JEWS LIKE JESUS ANY MORE
Well, the Good Lord must have had a reason.

IN THE END

The great American
head stone

_____

HE
WAS A GOOD GUY

_____

CODA

The wayfarer met the passerby
in death's champaign of flowers.
As the lint blew through their skulls
they spoke discreetly of the next world,
of the slobland to the left
and the awful coprolite above.
The words were impressive and muted.
Suddenly the one preoccupied
with his obsolete luetic eyeball
made a meaningless aside
in keeping with the serious scene.

(an image in mercury vapor, 1924)

POET'S CORNER

For Michael Heller

ODE ON ARRIVAL

a maquette

Here I am
in the house
of aesthetics,

in its great silence
where the air
is an abstraction.

I am in
the presence
of purity

and a great mass
like a sphinx behind me.

Sphinx,
are you there?

Best not to look
too closely lest
I lose my way,

my courage,
my self,
my everything.

This could be
the Great One.

Silly me, here I am
talking to
a figure of speech.

I'll be bold.
Sphinx, open up!
speak!

238

I SIT DOWN TO WRITE

Easy, old boy,
you don't have to
re-invent the wheel.

All you have to do
is head for *GRAVITAS*,
as in a mountain,

with a small truth,
co-opt rigor
and aim for the absolute,

but remember, you
have an assignation
with the spirit of man

and might put
your self
into a maquette.

A POEM IN THE MORNING

I must remember
            to write a poem in the morning
about America...
            a blockbuster.

I owe it.
            After all, who has suffered
as much as I?

SAILING ON WORDS

<u>absolute</u>, a little fellow
with a glass jaw

acting like a big boss
in a small precinct

serious as all hell.

<u>ABSOLUTE</u>, a poor sailor,
lost his anchor,

no sailing further,
no boat left.

no sailor either,
alas!

THE POET IN A GLASS OF PORT

Long live the creatures
of the sea and land,
the paramecium, the tiger,
for I have made

landing in Oporto
bound for 'Ewigkeit',
a pen in my hand
and crusty bread with
sweet butter for later.

THE BURDENS OF AMBIGUITY

If I think it,
it is so.

Presto,
a title appears,
Agony of the Axiom,
so profound it's
beyond description.

But the axiom
has no agony,
yet the idea
stands there
like a Titan.

What to do?
What to do?
What to do?

SHORT PSALM
AT MEMORIAL SERVICES
FOR ALLEN GINSBERG

Blessed be the poet
who places himself

squarely in
the public sector.

Blessed be
this predilection.

244

EPITAPH ON THE SHORT FORM

Here lies the Augustan temper,
a great lord

side by side
with the lark.

Pounds of cantos were unable
to quicken them.

THE AVANT GARDE ASKS AN APHORIST FOR A POEM OF NOT MORE THAN FIFTY-FIVE LETTERS

Well, how about

*a can
of worms?*

*a crock
of minnows?*

*a basket
of cockamamies?*

What about the packaging?

*Send them in
a hectare of space*

*on a ground
of character*

P.S. Mama Mia, that was no aphorist in the title!

OPERA

You have raised
a note
to the power
of an ego.

Bravissimo!

But why
are all
these people
singing?

THEME

How delightful to discover on Olympus
a god of silence
(and not a minor one either).

Hail Harpocrates!

How reassuring that you
are still here to protect us
against theorists.

ARCHETYPE

3 a.m.

telephone rings. . .

a young
trembly voice:

"I love you"

"What!"

*"Don't you
recognize
my voice?"*

"No"

"I'm a poet"

THE HUMORIST

Take one cliché/
re-work it

into original language/
add the spice

of personality
to bring out the truth

of your own time,
place and circumstance/

cook until hard-boiled/
refrigerate for an age/

If it's still you,
you're a poet.

SOME SERIOUS WORDS WITH THE CLICHÉ

Why so glum?
The devil's stripped you

of particulars?
So you're not singular!

but no one's
ever caught you

in flagrante delicto
with a trollop.

Look, you're on the lips
of every Tom,

Dick and Harry.
They're your kind

and you're their
Ultimate Reality.

So cheer up!
Never mind the poets.

THE PRANKSTER

Time blinked
and out rushed

the imagination
and in its wake

poetry
and in no time

banished
commonsense...

preferred orchids
to beef...

and danced to its own
capriccio and hubris.

Ho! Ho!
A new universe.

Then time
blinked again.

WRITTEN ON A WHITE CHALICE

Ptah
          who brought all things
even the gods
          into existence
by uttering
          their names,
the first linguist,

Ptah, you
          lover of words,
may you
          spend millions of years
sitting
          with your face to the North
and your eyes
          beholding happiness.

TWO GORGONS

"Is that you,
          poet,
     writhing
          in the underworld
     à la mode
               devouring
     the head
          of agony?"

"Critic,
          remember
     that when
               I was neither
     prophet
               nor mad
     I was only
          a minor bard."

REFLECTIONS ON MY MEDIUM

In the course of tracing the effect of certain forms on my poems, I stumbled onto an interesting connection to music. Needless to say, certain forms were more suitable to certain subject matter than others. The long line, for instance, was obviously better suited to developing a large representation, whereas the short line was better suited to making a point or an image. But apart from that, form kept sending a message that it had something of its own to express. A box shape, for example, gave a boxed-in feeling to a poem, and a poem shaped like a vertical rectangle looked severe. The longer the rectangle, the more uptight it looked, the very long finally looking constipated and puritanical. Breaking this mold and letting more space in between words and lines and changing their fixed positions immediately made a poem look more airy and graceful, easier on the eye, and seemed to liberate its lyrical spirit and restore it to its original impulse.

It was at this point that I perceived a connection to music, for when I extended the usual space between words, I became aware that I was registering them in the mind as individual entities and signalling that this was where (and now was when) the mind should meditate on them and summon their associations. And when I extended the space between lines, enough to make the reader wonder why, and moved them to the right or left, I became aware, for the first time, that the space between words and lines was not a null, as I had always assumed, that when I liberated it from its mold, it became expressive, a part of a poem's score, as it were, and when I did not hurry on, as usual, to the words but made myself stay with it, I became aware of a subliminal effect not unlike the silences in a Beethoven quartet when the spirit of the listener is summoned to resonate to the emotion being expressed in the notes. This resonance is anticipated by the composer in his tempo markings which instruct the performer just how much time he must allow between notes and is as much a part of the music as the notes themselves; is, in fact, the element necessary to give the music its fullest depth and special poignancy. All one has to do is to imagine a score with identical silences between notes, as in a popular song, to see that this is so.

What is one to make of this correspondence? Are the spaces between words and lines and the silence between notes really equivalents? I am not able to carry this further without becoming too abstract and diffuse, and there is not much point anyhow in claiming that they are. A better question to ask is what correspondences and connections are there between the intentions and effects of poetry and those of music, and how does the nature of their resources affect this. Not all kinds of poetry and music, naturally. I'd never be able to get out of such a jungle; just lyric poetry, which seems to me closest to the original poetic impulse (not to be confused with the impulse to write poetry, which everybody with an ego and a problem these days seems to have, or can be taught to simulate) and chamber music.

They both aim for the heart. Music travels straight to it and wrenches it. The effect is instantaneous. Not so poetry. Its lyrical impulse is tempered and modified at the very start by the nature of language, which places cognitive expectations on itself. To get to the heart, therefore, lyrical impulse has to sneak around them by a devious and complex route of word associations and timbres and cadences. Indirection is its very nature. Its effect, in fact, depends on it, and on subtlety and keeping under cover, otherwise the poet will be blamed for manipulating the reader, a kind of game between impulse and language in which language allows impulse to go its way but not openly and directly. In return, impulse gives up part of itself and takes on the burden of the cognitive demands of language.

Is it any wonder, therefore, that to the poet, the man of words, it is an endless wonder that music can achieve its effects without any words or visible devices of any kind; that its great power, in fact, comes from that fact. You'd think composers would feel that this great world of profound feeling in which the experience of music is the most existential in the arts because it is closest to pure being, is the best of all possible worlds. They do not. They are not quite satisfied. Apparently they sense something missing because they too in time turn to words, or assign a verbal, real-life meaning to music that is in no way realistic or verbal, pretending that what they had in mind was music's equivalent to this or that reality. Did not Beethoven himself end the Ninth Symphony with Schiller's 'Ode to Joy'? And did not Schubert set Goethe and any number of minor poets to music, not to mention Poulenc setting Apollinaire and Max Jacob? etc.

Perhaps we should not be surprised. After all, composers have minds as well as feelings and can't be expected to be content forever with only a world of feeling. And they too have been encoded with cognitive expectations and sooner or later feel the need for words.

To a poet, however, the coming together of music and poetry in an art song is not a blessed event. It is a union in which both lose, in my opinion: the music suffers in not being allowed to develop to its fullest on its own, and the poetry is diminished by being deprived of its own music and being taken over by the creative imagination of a different art, a different mind, and a different voice, and consigned to playing second fiddle to them. The only one who benefits is the singer. Only when the words in a poem are not good enough to stand on their own is there possible improvement. In that case, one can more or less disregard the words and experience just the music and the singer's voice. What a complex task the singer has to straddle both universes and to express both! Perhaps impossible.

If it is true that the composer does not feel quite complete at times without words, it is equally true that a good poet does not feel complete without music in his language. He hears it, in fact, as he works on a poem . . . a mutual yearning, as it were, for each other.

In this universe there is another force at work too, as I have mentioned, a counterpoint as it were, the silence between notes. I am drawn to this silence and keep coming back to it and feel there the power of the earliest existential pool from which wordless feeling and utterance come. I am not aware of this power in a poem in the visual blank between words but as soon as I voice the words to myself, I do sense something similar but faint.

Getting back now to the matter of form, it is safe to say that as long as people differ and as long as poets have imagination and a need to be original and distinctive, or simply to be themselves, and so long as the world keeps changing, one might add, along with the poet's experiences in it, there will be new forms; there have to be. But a new form can be very good for a poem, or middling, or a distraction and a bore. Obvious but necessary to say because experimentation has acquired so much prestige over the years and built up so much momentum that it tends to be honored whether it is good or bad.

In my own case it was not necessary to invent new forms because when I started to write, Williams and Cummings had just developed new forms with exciting possibilities for the new subject matter that I was getting into. Thus my attention was on other things in the making of a poem which were more difficult and problematic for me.

Nevertheless as time went on, some new forms did come to me but always in response to a particular content and to what I found visually pleasing and meaningful on the page. I liked best an airy, graceful look but that look is not suitable, of course, to every kind of poem. It would have turned my longish narrative poem, 'The Old Poet's Tale', into an ugly sprawl. What that poem needed was something that would express both control and movement. That was how I arrived at the unrhymed tercet, which expresses movement along a straight line ... which is what a narrative is.

On the other hand, I wrote 'Spring Fantasy', in a long and very thin, scraggly form, not more than one or two words to a line, because the poem is about a phonograph cartridge, which is oblong and narrow, and the ideas and images in the poem were tightly compressed and tangled the way a cartridge is. Too simplistic perhaps, but I thought that getting form and content to speak with one voice was more effective to this particular poem than an attractive appearance.

In general, form seems to matter somewhat in proportion to a poem's size. The very short poem is pretty much the same whatever form is used. Innovation does little for it. The longer a poem, the more it seems to need form, not only to keep it from disintegrating but also to express its subliminal bit about the over-all design and import. Innovation in form, therefore, may be an organic necessity for it.

It boils down then to what kind of poem one is writing. If, for example, one is being satirical, ironic, humorous, the whole point is vested in the content. Inventions in form in this case would be rather pointless, even distracting.

New forms are, in a sense, also the product of an attitude. A person to whom writing is an intellectual game or a form of play will be constantly motivated to invent new forms. Inventing them is part of the fun, the challenge, the interest. To a person to whom poetry is not a game, a preoccupation with innovations will be distasteful, demeaning in fact, because it puts devices ahead of real life in a poem, and at best reduces it to the dimensions of the device, and at worst, corrupts it. Cummings is a case in point. After one became used to his new devices and learned to live with them, they lost their newness and one saw that they were intended to shock his readers and make them admire him for a bold fellow. So far as the poetry was concerned, they served no purpose other than to draw attention to themselves as inventions. In other words, to serve themselves.

There's no denying that to the writer inventing new forms is an important and exciting business and often necessary to express his individuality and originality, but we must not delude ourselves that that is what is important to the reader. The reader who is not a literary historian is into a different experience when he reads a poem. To him the only thing that matters is the poem itself, its inherent interest and durability. In other words, the values to the poet of inventing something can not be passed on to the poem. That has to stand on its own merits.

Needless to say, the same is true for all the arts. New forms are constantly invented, nowhere more fearlessly and extensively than in modern painting. The ideas behind them, however, indicate that the painters' intentions have a far more profound and universal goal than the forms themselves. Kandinsky, for example, says "Everything has a secret soul, even a white trouser button glittering out of a puddle in the street." I too have a sense of this being true at the same time that I reject this as absurd. I try to come to grips with this, however. Is it that my nature as a poet has made me invest matter with an anima? Or simply that I've been conditioned by my reading? Both possibilities seem to me far weaker than Kandinsky's sense of matter, or mine.

Paul Klee goes further: "It is the artist's mission to penetrate that secret ground where the secret to all things lies." And Franz Marc goes all the way: "The goal of art is to break the mirror of appearance so that we may look being in the face." I am startled to find that a deep intuition in me agrees and makes me wonder whether this was one of the reasons why 'Objectivist' was never a satisfactory term for me. In any case the artist's mission stops there, but the philosophical mind can not. It goes on, for knowing the meaning of meaning itself is only a step from knowing the nature of being, which is only a step from knowing the meaning of being. But what a step! And what a frail thread of belief holds all this together.

Instead of moving forward I have moved backwards in time, to Mercurius, who the medieval alchemists believed was the mysterious spirit behind all things in nature. And further still to pre-historic man contemplating a rock. How strange to meet myself there, Mr. Rakosi, the pre-Adamite.

Connected to all this in some way I have not been able to figure out is abstraction. Abstraction is the mind's way of expanding meaning and transcending its own limitations. When an artist uses it, he tries to transcend the limitations of his medium. Gabo, for example, almost succeeded in discarding the very material from which his sculptures were made. The final product looks so pure, you'd think it was just a form in space, which of course it is, for the habitat of sculpture *is* space. In contrast, the habitat of poetry is not in space, it is not even in nature, it is all in the mind, and in what the mind has devised to express itself, language, a situation in which only good self-control and judgment and a commitment to humanity can protect poetry from the abuses of abstraction, which tends to get bloated if allowed a free hand.

INDEX OF TITLES

INDEX OF FIRST LINES

This publication was assisted by advance subscriptions to a clothbound
and paper edition. etruscan books thanks:

David Annwn
Spilios Argyropoulos
Arts Council Poetry Library
Fred Beake
Andrew Brewerton
Kelvin Corcoran
Peter Dent
Dillons, Southampton
John Freeman
David Greenslade
John Hall
Alan Halsey
Jeremy Hooker
Chris Hunt
Jesus College, Cambridge
Leslie Jones
Larry Lynch
Carl Major
James McGonigal
Rod Mengham
Edwin Morgan
Alice Notley
Tony and Nan Palmer
Performance Writing Dept., Dartington College of Arts
Ian Robinson
Pamela Robinson
Will Rowe
Heather Scott
Scottish Poetry Library, Edinburgh
John Seed
Iain Sinclair
Derek Slade
Stephen Stone
Gael Turnbull
Sam Ward
John Welch
Dr Malcolm Wiseman
University College Library, London
and 17 others.

If you would like to further assist the project for Carl
Rakosi's *Collected Works* please contact the publishers.